HEART
BEAT

HEART BEAT

ELIZABETH SCOTT

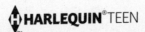 HARLEQUIN®TEEN

ISBN-13: 978-0-373-21096-1

HEARTBEAT

Printed in U.S.A.

HARLEQUIN®TEEN
www.HarlequinTEEN.com

To Astrolabe, for over fifteen years
of being a bright and joyful light in my life. I miss you every day.

I sit down with my mother. My smile is shaky as I tell her about my day.

"I think I did okay on my History test," I say. "Oh, and Olivia wore her new pair of false eyelashes, the ones I told you about. She was batting them around so much that a teacher stopped and asked if she had something caught in her eyes."

I laugh at the memory, and the sound is shaky too. "Olivia wasn't super happy about that."

There's the slightest movement, but it's not on Mom's face. Her face never changes. But under the skin of Mom's stomach…I don't want to look but I can't help it, because there my mother's skin is moving.

Because the baby is moving.

I close my eyes.

When I open them, Mom's stomach is stretched out and still.

"Emma, are you ready to go?" Dan says as he comes into the room, and I look up at him and nod.

"Did you two have a nice chat?" he says, bending over to kiss Mom.

I stare at him.

He must feel it because he straightens up, clearing his throat, and pats Mom's stomach. "Look how big he's getting. Lisa, he's growing so much."

Mom doesn't say anything, not even to that.

She can't.

She's dead. Machines are keeping her alive. They breathe for her. They feed her. They regulate her whole body.

My mother is dead, but Dan is keeping her alive because of the baby.

2

Dan and I don't talk on the ride home. As soon as I'm inside the house I head straight up to my room, and I lock the door.

I never used to have a lock, but then, I used to have Mom. I used to think that Dan cared about what I thought. What I wanted. What Mom would have wanted. This way, all the talks he used to try to have, right after Mom first died, can't happen. Or at least, he can talk, but I don't have to see him and can put on music or headphones or even fingers in my ears to shut him out. Just like he shut me out.

I don't have one of those wussy little turn-and-click locks. I have an actual lock, a bar with a padlock that I snap shut.

Closing out the world.

I put it in myself the day Dan told me what he was going to do to Mom. I walked out of the hospital, went to the hardware store and came home and put in the lock. My mother taught me how to do that. She believed women should know how to fix things. I'd seen her fix a broken toilet and watched her change the element in our hot water heater. She installed new locks on our doors when I was seven, after Olivia's family got robbed.

I go over to my window and open it. On the roof, Olivia grins at me through her blond hair and then comes over and pushes herself inside.

"How did you know I was out there?"

"I saw your hair when we came in. Also, your car down the road. Thanks for not parking...here."

"It makes things easier," she says. "And clearly, I need a wig. Oooh, I could get a bunch. Red hair, blue hair—"

"That wouldn't stand out at all."

She sticks her tongue out at me. "I'd get other ones too. Brown hair, black hair. I could be a spy, don't you think?"

"Spies have to use computers, Olivia."

"No, they don't. They go on missions. They have tech people do the computer stuff for them."

"Someone's been watching *Covert Ops*."

"Like you don't watch it too. You know you love it. You and your mom both think Sebastian is..." She trails off.

"Sebastian is cute," I say, and try not to think about how Mom and I used to watch the show together. "But he's also fictional, plus even spies on TV have to use earpieces and stuff—would you be willing to do that?"

"For Sebastian I would," she says, grinning, and then flops on my bed. "But I really wish I could be an old-fashioned spy. Like back when they had to write coded messages in invisible ink and speak a dozen languages."

"That sounds more like you," I say, and sit down next to her. "I—I saw the baby move today."

"Really?"

"Yeah."

"Emma," she says, squeezing my hand, "why do you even go to the hospital?"

"Because I can see her. Because I want at least one person to be there for Mom and not for the baby."

"Dan—"

"Dan wants the baby. You know it, I know it. If Mom was alive..." I stare at my dresser, at the photo of Mom and me. It was taken in Vermont when we went skiing. Mom is smiling and has one arm around me, holding me tight. It was the last vacation we took together, just her and me. She was thirty-five. I was ten.

She met Dan two weeks after we got back from Vermont. I was nice to him when I met him because he actually asked where I wanted to go to dinner when Mom suggested the three of us go out. I thought he was kind.

I also thought he loved Mom.

"Hey," Olivia says, and I look at her.

"She'd love you for being there," she says. "She does love you for being there. I know it."

I hug her, and Olivia hugs me back.

Dan knocks on my door. "Emma, you want some pizza? I made triple cheese."

Of course he did. Dan doesn't order food. He makes it. "The perfect man," Mom used to say. "He can cook, he makes the bed and he remembers to put the toilet seat down." Then she'd laugh and kiss him.

She loved him so much.

"I'm not hungry," I say.

"I'll leave it by the door," he says with a sigh. "Olivia, do you want me to leave you a slice too?"

Olivia looks at me. I shrug.

"Okay," Olivia says, and Dan says, "Thanks for coming today, Emma." Like he does every day. Like I'm doing it for him. Like I'm somehow in this with him.

I unbolt the door after five minutes. When I first started locking myself in, Dan would hang around and try to talk to me when I came out. I used to like how hard he tried, but I sure don't now. Not after what he's done to Mom. Now I wait until I'm sure he's gone.

Olivia eats most of the pizza and then says she has to get home to make sure her parents eat.

"Wish me luck," she says. "Prying their handheld whatevers away from them for longer than thirty seconds makes them both go into withdrawal. See you tomorrow?"

"Yeah. You don't have to go out on the roof to leave, you know."

"I know," she says. "But if I use the front door or try to go out any other way, I'll see Dan. And I know he'll ask me about you. He did the last time I left that way. I think he—well, I think he's worried about you, you know?"

"Why? Because my mother is dead and he's kept her body alive so he can try to save his precious son? Because I have to see her lying there—" I break off and open the window for Olivia.

Olivia hugs me again and then leaves. After she does, I

close my window and get into bed. It's early, but I don't care. In bed, I can look at my ceiling. It's yellow and the color is swirled around so there are a million patterns and shapes to get lost in. Mom painted it last year even though the doctor didn't want her "exerting" herself because she'd just had a blood clot taken out of her leg.

"Think about this instead of that boy," she'd said when I came in and lay down on the bed to look at it.

"I can't," I'd said. "Anthony broke my heart."

"I know," she'd said, lying down next to me. "But one day he won't matter."

"He said I was lovely." I'd looked up at the ceiling.

"They all say something like that," she'd told me. "Trust the one who takes his time saying it."

"Dan said he was falling in love with you on your second date."

"Dan's different," she'd said. "He's older, for one thing. And so am I. It's…you won't believe me, but one day Anthony will just be a memory and it won't hurt when you see him at all, I promise."

She was right. I wish I'd told her that. I could have. Anthony was nothing to me ages before she died.

I wish I could tell Mom something, anything, and have her really hear it.

"I miss you," I whisper, and listen to Dan moving around downstairs. If I close my eyes, I can pretend I hear Mom, that this is just another night.

That she's still here.

3

Dan drives me to school in the morning. He has done this since he and Mom got married, and I used to like it although I did start to ride with Olivia when she got her license.

That stopped when Mom died. I wanted Dan to remember I was around. I wanted him to remember Mom.

Like, Mom worried about my grades. Not that they weren't good enough, but that I was working too hard. Dan told her that in order to grow up I had to be allowed to make my own choices.

Oh yes, Dan and his choices.

We drive to school in silence. At seventeen, I'm old enough to get my license, but the waiting list to get into any of the driver's ed classes within half an hour of the house stretches out for months. I'd planned to put my name on a list last year but never got around to it.

Last year, before everything happened, Dan promised that over the summer he'd teach me how to drive and then I could just go get my license.

I don't want him teaching me to drive now. What if something happens? What if I get hurt? If my body stops working, my brain stops functioning? Would he have machines keep me alive in case his son might one day need something? A lung, a kidney, bone marrow?

But I do ride in the car with him to school. I do it because it means he will have to pick me up afterward. That he will have to see me, that he will take me to see Mom. He works at home, so he can do that.

Or at least, he used to work at home. I don't know if he still does, or if all the database consulting he did stopped when Mom did. Lately, he hasn't mentioned any two-hour phone calls to talk someone through using a new feature he's built.

But then, I haven't asked. I don't want to talk to him.

He was going to stay home with the baby, and Mom was going to go back to work. That was their plan. She was an assistant manager at BT&T bank. They sent flowers when she died. They didn't send anything for the baby. Maybe they didn't know what to do about it, but maybe they heard about what Dan's doing and think he's keeping a dead woman alive so he can get what he wants.

If they do, I love them for that. I mean, I know it's a baby and it's partly Mom, but I wish Dan had just once thought about what Mom would have wanted. It was so easy for him to choose to keep her here, dead, and it's so hard for me to think about, much less see.

"I got a call from your AP History teacher about how you're doing in class. Maybe we should talk about it," Dan says as we stop, one car in the many that are waiting to snake into the high school. Mostly freshman and sophomores get out here. Juniors get rides with their friends who have licenses or, better yet, get their own and a car to go with it.

I could get a ride with Olivia, but I don't.

"See you later," I tell Dan and get out of the car. I won't talk to him about school just like I won't ride to school with Olivia anymore. If I did, then Dan would get to feel like things are normal and they're not. They are so not. Not while Mom is still...

The tears hit me hard, hot pressure behind my eyes, in my throat, in my chest. It's hard to breathe, to see, to think.

I look down at the ground and walk, blinking hard once they've started to spill down my face.

I cry without making a sound now. I have cried soundlessly, wordlessly, since I stood with Dan at the hospital and heard, "I'm sorry, but..."

Dan cried openmouthed then, sobbing, yelling his grief for everyone to see. I tried to hug him. I felt for him because I thought he loved her, because we were in the same place, because she was gone and he felt the gaping hole that had been born too, a Mom-shaped space in the universe.

He didn't hug me back. He didn't even seem to see me.

And then the doctor told him about the baby.

"Hey," Olivia says, and I know it's her because I would

know her voice anywhere. We've been friends since first grade, and we've been through period trauma, boy crap, bad hair, her parents and their ways. And now Dan and his baby.

"Hey," I say. I wipe my eyes and look at her. "How's the car?"

Olivia makes a face at me but also wraps an arm around my shoulders, steering me toward our lockers. Her parents gave her a fully loaded convertible when she got her license, one with a built-in music player, phone, navigation system— you name it, the car had it. Could do it, and all at the touch of a button.

Olivia sold the car—through the one newspaper left in the area, which is basically just ads—and bought a used car. It's so old all it has is a CD player and a radio. We bought CDs at yard sales for a while, but all we could get was old music, which we both hate, and the radio is just people telling you that what they think is what you should think, so we mostly just drive around in silence.

It used to bother me sometimes but now I like it. The inside of my head is so full now that silence is…I don't know. There's just something about knowing Olivia is there, and that we don't have to talk. That she gets it. Gets me and what's going on.

Her parents were unhappy about the car, though. Really unhappy, actually, but then there was a big crisis with one of their server farms at work and by the time they surfaced for air they hadn't slept in four days. And when they said, "Olivia, that car was a gift," she said, "Yes, it was. A gift, meaning something freely given, for the recipient to use as she wanted to, right?"

As we hit her locker, we pass Anthony, and he says, "Ladies," bowing in my direction. A real bow too, like it's the nineteenth century or something.

"Ass," Olivia says.

"A donkey is actually not as stupid as people believe. However, you are entitled to your own beliefs about asses. And me." He looks at me. "Hello, Emma."

I sigh. "Hi, Anthony."

"If you ever want to talk about your grades, do know that I'm here."

I can't believe I ever thought the way he talked was interesting. It's just stupid, like he's too good to speak like a normal person. "I know, Anthony."

"I really would like to be of assistance to you. I believe in helping everyone. I'm talking to Zara Johns later. I think she feels threatened by the fact that I've been asked to help her organize the next school blood drive." Translation: he's butted in, and Zara's furious.

"Either that or she just doesn't like you. Emma, let's go," Olivia says, slamming her locker shut, and we head for mine.

"You okay?" she says, and I nod. Anthony doesn't bother me at all anymore, just like Mom said would happen. I look at him and feel nothing. Well, some annoyance, but then, who wouldn't after listening to him talk?

Of course, I didn't always think that he was annoying. I open my locker, deciding not to go down the Anthony road, and hear the guy next to me say, "No way! I mean, every-one knows what'll happen to Caleb if he steals another car."

Olivia and I glance at each other. If Anthony is the ass end of the smart part of the school, Caleb Harrison is the ass end of the stupid part. He's a total druggie and three years ago, when we were freshmen, he came to school so high he couldn't even talk. I heard that stopped last year, but then, as soon as school got out, his parents sent him off to some "tough love camp," which is rich-people code for boot-camp rehab.

He came back seemingly off drugs but newly into steal-ing cars. He started by grabbing them at the mall and park-ing them in a different spot, but then he stole a teacher's car.

And then he graduated to a school bus. It was empty at the time, but still, I heard that got him a couple of weeks in juvie, or would have except for his parents, who intervened. I guess now he's taken yet another step forward and by lunchtime, I know what Caleb stole.

His father's brand-new, limited-edition Porsche. And he didn't just steal it. He drove it into the lake over by the park, drove right off the highway and into the water. The police found him sitting on the lake's edge, watching the car sink. They were able to pull it out, but water apparently isn't good for the inside of a Porsche.

"You think he'll go to jail this time?" Olivia asks as we sit picking at our lunches. I love that we have lunch together this semester, but it's the first lunch block, and it's hard to face food—especially cafeteria food—at 10:20 in the morning.

"I guess it depends on his parents," I say. "Last time they

talked to the judge or whatever. They'll probably just ship him off again. He must hate them, though."

"Yeah. To sit by the lake and watch the car sink like that—"

"Exactly."

"Even when my parents are sucking their lives away with all their computer crap, I'd never do anything like mess with their stuff," she says. "How can you hate someone who raised you, who loves you so—" She breaks off.

"Dan didn't raise me," I say tightly. "And he doesn't love me. Or Mom."

Olivia nods and I think about hate. I understand what can make someone do what Caleb did, although I don't think a bored, rich druggie really gets hate. Not real hate.

I do, though. If there were something I could do to Dan that would hurt him, I'd do it.

4

The rest of school is like school always is. I sit, I pretend to listen, avoid my AP History teacher's attempt to try to talk to me after class and wait for the final bell to ring.

I used to like school. I was the person—along with Anthony—who got A's on everything and so wrecked any possible grading curve. I did extra credit assignments for fun. I went out and did research about authors we were going to read. I learned about minor historical figures we'd discussed in passing.

Last summer, I audited a biology class at the community college to make sure everything I'd learned in Advanced Bio stayed in my head. I was going to do the same thing with chemistry this summer, and maybe something in literature too.

I was a great student. The kind of student everyone hates, actually. I didn't make friends in my classes, I had acquaintances that I blew away at everything, but I didn't care. I wanted great grades, the best grades, and I had Olivia, who was in regular classes and who knew there was a list of the top one hundred colleges out there but had no idea which was number one. Or eight. Or forty.

I knew what the number one school was, and I knew I couldn't go there because one year of tuition cost an amount that was enough to support a family (or possibly two) for that year and they were stingy with scholarships, but I wanted a scholarship to one in the top ten. I wanted to be the best, not just for the scholarship I'd need to go to a great college, but because I could be.

A lot of the time, I was. The best, I mean.

At school, anyway. Personally, my social life was...well, it was pretty poor. A few kisses at a few parties. Anthony.

Very poor, really.

I didn't mind. My dad—my real dad—was a history professor, and I wanted to be like him. Ever since I was little, that's what I wanted. To be what my dad was. To see my mother's face when I got my PhD in history.

I don't care about school at all now. I sit in class and if I get called on, I say, "I don't know." I don't do my homework and the leeway I got at first is gone. I'm getting F's on quizzes. On tests. I'm still ignored by my classmates, but now it's because I've fallen so far behind I'll never get back to where I was. I'm no threat anymore.

I have a twenty-page paper on the New Deal that's beyond late. I haven't written a word of it.

I'm not going to. I don't care about school right now, and if I ever do again, I'll never care about history. It's nothing but studying things that have happened. That are gone.

History is full of death, and I've had enough of that.

5

It took almost two years for my mother to get pregnant. Two years of planning, of Dan smiling and talking, hoping. Of Mom going to the fertility doctor's office over and over again.

Of me hearing her crying sometimes.

"I'm sad," she'd say when I asked, and I would watch her, so drained-looking, and wonder why she was doing it.

But then Dan would show up, dry her tears, kiss her, and she'd smile and I'd know why. She wanted him to be happy. She loved him.

So she tried. And tried.

And tried.

She was pregnant with me when she married my dad. She didn't know it, but she was. She used to say I was such a quiet baby that she didn't even know I was there until her clothes started getting tight.

"Of course," she'd say, "you made up for it with the colic, but still, you were worth it." And then she'd kiss my forehead or my cheek. She used to talk about how easy it was, being pregnant with me, before she started trying for Dan.

Before trying to get pregnant took over her life.

My dad named me. His parents, who'd died when he was fourteen, left him in the care of his aunt Emma because one set of his grandparents was dead and the others were both well on their way to drinking themselves there. Emma loved history, just like my father, and took out a second mortgage on her house to send him to graduate school. She got sick with a cold the day before he got his doctorate and died of a massive internal infection a week after she saw him get it.

Dan's parents are dead, which is the only thing he and my dad have in common, besides the whole being married to Mom part. My mother's parents are both alive, but they live in Arizona and I've only met them twice. Both times were awful. They basically spent the entire visit telling my mother that she was such a disappointment and she needed to "turn herself into someone better." The second time, Mom told them that maybe they needed to fix themselves and then we left. They didn't try to get in touch with her again and when she died, they called and left a message.

I think that's why Mom was such a great mom. In spite of her parents, or maybe because of them, she taught herself how to love.

And she did.

She loved so much, and she loved with everything, with her soul. I wanted to be like that.

I don't anymore.

Mom did a lot of stuff for Dan, but what she did to get that baby...some of it sounded pretty gruesome. Painful, even. I once heard her tell Dan, "I don't think I can do it. I just... my body is like this *thing* now."

"We'll talk to the doctor," Dan said. "He did warn us that with that blood clot you had, things could be even riskier. And I know being on the drugs is hard. So if you're this un-happy..."

"No, no," Mom said, but of course she'd say that. She loved Dan. She knew how much he wanted a baby. She knew that because she was over forty when they started trying, her best chances of having a baby—"The dream baby," she used to say with a smile—lay with drugs and testing and all kinds of stuff. And risk. So much risk.

Dan began setting up a nursery in the guest bedroom about thirty seconds after the clinic called to say it looked like she was pregnant, and I can remember Mom saying, "Dan, it hasn't even been a day yet. I don't want you to hope too much."

"Don't be afraid," Dan had said. "I know it's true." He grinned at me as I stood in the corner of the already-changing guest room. "You're going to have a brother or a sister, Emma!"

"But if it hasn't even been a day—" I said, and then broke off as Mom looked at me, her face full of love and pleading.

"You need help with what you're doing?" I said to him,

and helped Dan box up the extra linens in the closet, sat with him while he drew up plans for what would go where and Mom sat, listening to him and smiling a little.

She was pregnant for real then, finally. But it was a hard pregnancy from the start. She was sick all the time, so much that she lost weight. Dan made her favorite meals to try to get her to eat but it didn't help much.

And then, in the second month, she had some spotting and had to go the hospital. Dan rushed there from the house so fast he forgot to call the school and tell them to find me and tell me what was going on.

I still remember coming home and finding Mom in bed.

"What happened?" I said. "Is something wrong with the baby?"

"No, everything's fine," Mom said. "I just—I was bleeding some before and—" She broke off, her voice cracking, her eyes filling with tears.

"Lisa, honey, don't cry. You're okay. You're going to be fine," Dan said, and Mom nodded but she didn't look like she believed him. She looked scared.

I waited until Dan left and sat down next to her. "Mom, are you okay about the baby? Dan talks about it all the time, but you don't and I'm wondering if—"

She squeezed my hand and said, "Emma, honey, I know what I want. I just…it was hard to get here. But now I am. I beat all the odds—over forty, all the drugs, the warnings about the clot—ugh, I already went over it. And over it."

She touched her stomach and I kissed her cheek and lay beside her.

"I could get used to this," I said a while later, stretching out with one foot to try to pull the TV remote up toward me.

"Not me," she said. "I'd like to be able to get up and move around. I feel trapped just lying here. I mean, if I could paint your ceiling after the clot came out, why can't I walk downstairs?"

"I heard that," Dan called from the hallway. "No rest, no chocolate cake."

"Meanie," Mom said, grinning, but she was tapping her toes against the bed, like she heard a song and was following the beat. Like she wanted to move to it.

She was able to get out of bed after a week, and everything after that went okay. She still got sick, but not as much, and she started to finally gain some weight.

And then, on a Wednesday morning, after I'd already left for school with Olivia, she went to grab a piece of toast in the kitchen and fell down.

That was it.

That's how she died.

She was getting breakfast, something she did every day, something normal, and her body just…stopped.

Dan ran right over to her and performed CPR until the ambulance came. She wouldn't—couldn't—open her eyes. Couldn't feel anything when she was touched. Couldn't talk.

She'd had a massive stroke caused by an embolism in her brain, the kind that—

The kind that you don't come back from.

Mom was gone when she hit that floor. CPR kept her lungs going for a while, and then surgery and tubes and machines to try to figure out what was going on took over. And then the doctor came out and said, "I'm sorry, but she's gone."

"Gone?" Dan said. "But she was breathing! I was with her. She was breathing!"

I tried to hug him, and then the doctor drew him aside. I found out later he told Dan that Mom was brain-dead, that without medical intervention she wouldn't be breathing, that her heart wouldn't be beating. That the baby was still alive and Dan could have everything turned off now—and let Mom go—or keep her hooked up to machines until the baby was old enough to maybe live on its own.

Mom never knew what happened to her. That's what I have to hold on to. That at least it was fast. That whatever pain there was didn't last long. That she reached for a piece of toast and left forever.

Except she's still here—alive but not alive—and I wonder if part of her is trapped in her broken body. A prisoner of the baby swimming around inside her.

I think of how scared she was and wonder if this was what she saw coming. If she knew that no matter what happened to her, Dan would pick the baby—that Dan would choose his baby over her. Over the family we'd had. Did she know that he would look me in the eye and say, "Your mother would want this," even after I'd lain next to her in bed and heard how restless and scared not being able to move made her?

How having to lie still made her feel trapped.

Sometimes I hope she's gone, that she's in heaven look-ing down at all of this, but I've felt the weight of her hand in mine every day since she died. I've watched her fade, become smaller despite all the nutrients piped into her, the baby taking all it can.

She isn't gone. Not like she should be.

My mother's name was Lisa Davis Harold, and she was strong and beautiful. She was a person, she had her own thoughts, and I remember that. I remember how she was. Who she was.

I remember her.

I'm the only one who does.

6

At the hospital, Dan always goes in and says hi to Mom first.

Actually, he wanted "us" to go in and "say hello together," but the first and only time he asked me that, the night after I'd lain in bed, thinking of my mother lying in the hospital kept alive for the baby—his baby—I said, "There isn't an us. There's you, and then there's me."

"But we're family."

"Were," I said. "Go see what you're here for. And then I'm going to see Mom."

"I'm here every bit as much for your mother as I am for the baby."

"I know. After all, if her body can't be kept alive long enough, your baby won't survive, will it?"

"Emma, that's not—"

"It's not? Then what is it?"

"It's what your mother would want."

I slapped him. Right there, in the hospital.

Security was called, but Dan said nothing was wrong, that we were "just struggling with our loss" and that he'd sit with me outside for a while.

He did walk outside with me, and he actually put a hand on my arm and said, "Emma, please. I don't think you're seeing—"

"Don't touch me," I said. "Don't try to sell me your story. Mom loved you, I know that. You can kick me out of the house, send me to live with Mom's parents, maybe boarding school. Take your pick."

"I'd never do that. You're my family. Don't you know that? Don't you know I love you like you were my own—"

"Go see her," I said, cutting him off and making sure I was out of his reach.

"You should come too."

"I don't want to see her with you."

"Emma—" he said and then sighed.

So that's how I got to see Mom on my own. Dan goes in first while I sit in the waiting room outside the ICU, and then he goes and drinks some of the hospital's sludge coffee. I don't think he likes it, but then I don't care what Dan thinks or likes anymore.

He's in there now, doing his thing, and I'm staring at the ceiling. I did homework for the first few days, more out of numbness than anything else, and then I realized it was easier to just sit and look at the ceiling like I do at home. To think about how she'd painted it, to think about her, and not where I am.

To not think about Mom tethered to a bed by machines and IVs and the lump in her belly.

One of the volunteers comes in with the magazine cart. The thing is a joke because the hospital never has any new magazines. They just replace the old issues with slightly less old issues. But then I suppose most people in here aren't really that concerned with what's going on in the world.

I know I'm not.

The magazine cart squeaks as it comes over to the last table in the room, the one that's at the far end of the bank of chairs where I like to sit. Not that there are a lot of people in the waiting room today. Or any day. The ICU is not a place where people come to stay for a long time. Not usually, anyway, but my mother is "special."

The tears come again and I blink, watch the ceiling waterfall into little pieces as my throat gets tight.

I don't want to see Mom like this, and I pinch the bridge of my nose hard. It makes my head hurt but stops the tears.

Mom used to do it whenever she thought she might cry. She hated to cry, and I can remember how, on the day she married Dan, she sat there getting her hair done and pinching her nose over and over so she wouldn't cry and mess up her makeup.

I was part of the ceremony. Mom and I walked down the aisle together, and before Mom and Dan became husband and wife, Dan asked for my permission to be part of our family. He said, "I'm so happy to have found you and your mother and I promise I'll always look out for you. I'll always want what you do, I'll always believe in you."

"Liar," I mutter, and wipe my eyes.

I look away from the ceiling and see Caleb Harrison staring at me.

It's definitely him. We aren't in any of the same classes but he's in the lunch block Olivia and I share and I've seen him getting food, shoving his perfectly wavy blond hair off his face as he waits to pay.

"What did you just say?" he says, and if it wasn't for the snarl in his voice—plus the fact that he steals cars (and now apparently drives them into lakes as well)—he'd be cute.

More than cute, even.

But he does sound angry, and under his hair, blond curls falling all over his face, his eyes are narrowed and very pissed-off looking.

"Nothing," I mutter, and he grunts and turns away. I stare at his back and only then start to wonder why he's here.

And why does what I said matter to him? Does he really

think I would be sitting here, in the waiting room outside the ICU, and somehow be thinking about him? I mean, *really?* Yes, everyone knows who he is, but it's not like he's the kind of guy I'd go for. And besides, what do I have to be afraid of from him anyway? From anyone?

"Hey," I say. "Can I have a *Women's One?*"

He turns back around. *"What?"*

"A *Women's One* magazine," I say, and he really does think I was sitting here thinking about him, because he's glaring at me and plucking a magazine off the cart like it's diseased.

"What's your problem?" he says, tossing it to me. It lands on the floor by my feet. "If you have something you want to say to me—"

"Emma," Dan says, coming into the room, "you can go in now."

"Great," I say and get up, step on the magazine and then push past Caleb Harrison like he isn't there.

Mom is…she's the same as she's been since she was put in this room. She's still, so still, and I sit and look at her closed eyes, at her slightly downturned mouth. At the tube going into it.

Her skin is strange-colored, almost waxy-looking, and her hand is warm but limp in mine.

"It wasn't much of a day," I tell her, and look around. The unit Mom's in has huge open windows by every door—I don't know why—but I can see people in other rooms. Most of them are sitting like I am, hunched by a bedside. A few are weeping. A few are just staring, lost-looking.

I look away, look back at Mom. "I turned in my paper on the New Deal," I say. "And we've started a new book in English that I like a lot. Oh, and I got an A on my Algebra

II quiz." I talk and talk, spinning a story of a day filled with academic success. Filled with lies.

Part of it is because I am looking at her and I want her to think everything is okay even though I know she can't hear me.

Part of it is because part of me thinks that maybe she can, that despite everything the doctor said she will somehow open her eyes and say, "Emma, I know something's wrong. I can hear it in your voice. Start talking, okay?"

Yes.

Yes, I want to talk about it so much; I love you and I miss you and I wish you were here but not like this, I don't want you here like this and I know I'm seventeen but I don't want you to be gone. I want you to open your eyes and tell me everything is going to be okay. I want you to squeeze my hand and tell me something, anything. I want to hear your voice, not the machines that beep all around us.

"Mom," I whisper, and kiss her hand, pressing my cheek to it, eyes closed as I imagine.

I feel movement, a slight shift in her but I know it's not her. It's the baby.

"Why did you do it, Mom?" I ask. "Why did you try so hard for this when it was so hard on you? When the risks were so many? When you cried so much? When you ended up—when now you're here?"

I hear Dan's voice as he comes back into the ward. He always says hello to everyone, like he's so friendly. Like he's actually thinking about anything other than himself.

I open my eyes and see a magazine cart in front of the door.

And I see Caleb Harrison staring at me again.

"Hey there," Dan says to him as he comes to the room. "I saw you earlier, right?"

Caleb nods, looking at him and then my mother. I see him stare at her stomach.

Dan walks into the room. "Lisa, Emma and I are both here now, and I thought we'd all talk for a little while before we have to go." He pats Mom's stomach. "I was thinking today we could talk about names."

"No," I say, and Dan looks at me.

Caleb, still standing in the doorway, looks at me too, and Dan glances at me, then at him, and says, "We don't need anything to read now, thanks."

Caleb shrugs and moves off, the cart squeaking as he goes.

"You know him?" Dan says.

"No, but it's not every day you see a girl sitting with her dead mother, is it? People would stare at that, don't you think?"

"Emma, honey, your voice—"

"She can't hear me."

"The baby can, though, and I don't want—"

I stand up so fast that I'm dizzy for a second. I don't want to hear more. I can't hear more.

"I don't feel good," I say. "Can we go?"

"I really was hoping we could talk about names. I'd like for you and I to…" He sighs. "Your little brother is in there, Emma. He's in there and he's fighting to stay alive."

I walk out of the room then. I stop at the nurses' station and ask to use the phone. I hear Dan come out when he realizes I'm not coming back. I hang up the phone.

"Emma," he says, but I pretend I can't hear him and walk out. He follows me, of course.

"You're hurting your mother," he says when we're waiting for the elevator. "She wanted this baby. She'd want you to be part of this. She'd be so sad to see how you're acting."

I stay silent. I stay silent all the way to the car, all the way to the house. I don't think of it as home anymore.

"You say what she wants. What she thinks, what she feels," I say when we get there. "She can't do anything now, and it's all because of you and what you want. So don't tell me how she feels, because she *can't* feel. She's dead. She died trying to have your baby, and if you want to think about feelings and Mom, how do you think she feels about that? How do you think being dead makes her feel?"

"Emma," Dan says, and then "Emma!" but I'm out of the car and heading down the driveway, heading toward the car I know is waiting there.

The lights turn on as I reach it, and I open the passenger door and get in.

"Thank you," I say, and Olivia nods, squeezing my hand before we drive off.

9

The phone at Olivia's house is blinking when we get in but she ignores it, sits me down in her parents' gleaming steel kitchen and puts a peanut butter sandwich in front of me.

"Just don't let me see you destroy it," she says, putting a bag of corn chips next to me, and then goes over to the phone.

I hear her talking while I'm opening the sandwich and putting corn chips on top of the peanut butter.

"No, she called me from the hospital, and I said I'd come get her. I—look, Dan, I think she just needs some decompression time. You know?"

I love Olivia. Not just for talking to Dan for me, but for a million little things. Like, she was okay that my mom loved peanut butter and corn chip sandwiches even before I was. I thought the idea was disgusting until I found myself wandering around the house three nights after she reached for toast and then broke. I was thinking about her, the things she did, like how she always had to put her wallet in her purse before she'd put anything else in or how much she hated peas.

I was wandering, remembering, and I was alone. Dan was sleeping peacefully, no doubt dreaming of his baby.

I thought about those sandwiches.

I made one the way she always did, first pressing the slices of bread and peanut butter together, and then taking them apart to put the chips on before smooshing it back together, and it was good. As I ate it, for a moment I swear I could almost see her. Picture her smiling at me.

"Sure, she'll call later," Olivia says. "Okay. Bye."

She comes back to the table, one arm extended. I hand her the chips and smile as she heads toward the pantry, eyes averted from my sandwich.

"It's not that bad. I've seen those gel things your parents eat."

"True," she says, coming back to the table and sitting down.

"You can see the sandwich now since you're sitting here, you know."

"Yeah, I know. What happened?"

I tell her.

"Oh," she says when I'm done. "Names, huh? He must really think the baby's going to make it."

"I guess. All it has to do is lie there and suck everything out of Mom that's pumped in until it can survive long enough to live in an incubator."

"Emma," Olivia says, picking up my plate and walking

over to the shiny steel sink. "You know the baby's not a bug or anything. It's your brother."

"Half. And it's—Mom is dead and it's not and I try not to see it but sometimes it moves and Mom's—she's just lying there, you know? Her body is only there for the baby and Dan chose that. He said he loved her, that he'd do anything for her. What kind of love is that, Olivia? Would you want someone to keep your dead body breathing with tubes and machines because they wanted something from you?"

I'm yelling by the end and Olivia has come back to the table and puts her arms around me.

"I'm sorry," she says. "I don't—my parents—our family's not like it was for you and your mom. And the baby, it'll never even know her. That's so strange and awful."

"When Dan finally gets around to thinking about that, he'll probably just say it's proof that science can work miracles and it's how Mom would have wanted it." By the time I'm done talking, I'm shaking so hard my teeth are chattering.

"I want to fix it for you, you know?" Olivia says. "You're so angry, Emma. And I don't know if it's with Dan or your mom."

"Dan. Definitely Dan."

"And the baby."

"I—look, I do get that it didn't choose for Mom to die. But she did, you know? And the doctors say the embolism didn't happen because she was pregnant but it's just…" I swallow. "There was that clot and everything else—she was so scared, you know, so scared, and now I see her every day and try not to wonder if she'll wake up even though I know she can't. That she won't."

"Maybe you should talk to someone."

"Dan said that too," I say. "What's a shrink going to tell me that I don't already know? My mother's dead and I miss her. I'm angry at Dan for keeping her body alive so the baby he wants so badly can maybe survive. Mom would hate being trapped like she is and I can't—won't—forgive him for it. I can't forgive the baby either, and maybe that makes me awful, but I don't care."

"You really are angry. Like, I'm worried about you angry."

I shrug and stare at the table again. Olivia knows me and she's right. I am angry. I am so angry I feel like it's all I am.

"At least I'm angry for a reason. At least I'm not running around stealing cars for fun like Caleb Harrison. I saw him at the hospital today. Twice, actually."

"Wow, so it is true," Olivia says.

"What?"

"I heard his parents got him some emergency hearing and he got assigned community service for the thing with his dad's car," she says. "You know, picking up trash and stuff. But I guess he's at the hospital instead. What did he say?"

"Nothing," I say, thinking of his, *What's your problem?* and his stares. The second one was the worst. The way he was just looking at me and Mom, and how he must have seen me lying there, resting my head on her hand.

"Nothing? You sure?"

"How do you know what happened to him, anyway? It's

not like you'd have found out by going anywhere near a computer, so that means you talked to someone and that means…"

"Yes, I saw Roger," she says, and blushes. "But it's not what you think. I was getting gas and when I went to pay for it, he was inside getting a soda and we talked for a minute."

"Uh-huh. So you were getting gas."

"Yep."

"Even though you got it two days ago and you've only driven to school and back since."

"All right, fine," she says, mock-slapping my arm. "I saw his car in the parking lot and I might have wanted to see him, and I did but it was no big deal. Okay?"

"How long did you talk to him?"

"Awhile."

I grin at her. She stares at me for a moment and then grins back. "I know! We talked! Do you think he likes me? I really want him to like me."

"What's not to like?"

"The fact that most people think I'm a freak because I don't use computers or any of that stuff."

"Olivia, we go to school with people who steal buses. And their father's car. Oh, and that guy who always wears the same brown shirt. You're not a freak."

"Well, not compared to Caleb Harrison. Or Dennis and his shirt thing," she says. "But neither of them have social lives and I'd like one."

"You have one. You talk to people in your classes. You dragged me to parties after the horrorfest that was Anthony.

You went out with Pete last year. If you ever started using technology, you'd rule the school in a week."

"Nice try," she says, and grins at me. "Roger said I have nice hair, but what does that mean? It just lies there."

"Olivia, you *do* have nice hair."

"It's flat."

"You'd like Caleb's hair," I say, and she blinks at me.

"What?"

"I just—it's wavy and stuff. Like how you're always saying you want yours to be."

"I thought you didn't talk to him."

"I didn't."

"But you noticed his hair."

"We were in the same room, Olivia. He was about two feet away from me. It was hard not to see him."

"He's cute," she says, and now I stare at her.

"No, not I think he's *cute* cute," she says. "Scary druggies don't do it for me. But a lot of girls think he's hot."

"Not the ones in my classes!"

"No, you all think guys like Anthony are hot. Caleb's got that whole quiet loner thing going, plus he has the cheekbone/eye/hair trifecta."

When I stare at her she says, "Awesome face, great eyes, amazing hair. A trifecta. What are you learning in your classes?"

"Not that."

"Oh, right. How's the New Deal paper coming anyway?"

"It's not."

She looks at me and then says, "For real?"

I shrug.

"I know you haven't been buried in books like usual but I thought you wanted to go to one of those top ten schools. I thought you and Anthony were neck and neck to see who could have the best ranking and SAT score and all that stuff."

"Yeah, we were."

Olivia frowns and starts to say something else, but her parents come in. They are both blond, like she is, but that's pretty much where any similarity stops. They work in IT support and their life—their world, in fact—is computers. I have never seen one of them without something that isn't electronic in one hand. It reminds me of how Olivia and I started the whole hanging out on my roof thing.

A few years ago, they gave her some sort of "does every-thing and can organize everything" gadget for her birthday and she came over, climbed up the trellis on the side of our house onto our roof, knocked on my window (and scared the crap out of me), and when I came out onto the roof, she cried and we talked. And then I threw her gift off the roof.

Mom calmed Olivia's parents down, then calmed Olivia down, and then gave her a birthday gift from "me and Emma" and put foot rungs on the trellis so she could get up onto the roof easier. Since then, it was something we did once in a while for fun, but since Mom died, it's the only way she comes to see me.

Her mother closes the door while typing out a message on some impossibly tiny thing, never looking up. Her father, who entered first, is using a strange-looking square, holding it in one hand and touching it with a plastic stylus, frowning as images flicker in and out.

"This cube isn't maximizing its storage capability or its potential speed," he says. "It feels like more of a design idea than an actual product."

Olivia rolls her eyes at me, gets up and gets two energy drinks out of the fridge. "Hi, Mom. Hi, Dad."

"How are you?" her dad says as her mother smoothes a hand over Olivia's shoulder. "You have a good day?"

"Yeah," Olivia says, and her Mom's device starts to beep.

"Have you eaten?" her mother says, and Olivia rolls her eyes again.

"Yes. You?"

Her mother nods, and Olivia looks at her dad, who flushes. "I'm going to," he says. "But the cube came in and I wanted to see it. I'll eat later."

"Something without caffeine or the word *Energy!* in it?"

Her dad grins at her. "Yes. And hey, we have a little more work to do, but then we're going to watch a movie."

"By yourselves?" Olivia says. "Without anything electronic in hand? Will you be all right?"

"You," Olivia's mother says, and kisses her cheek. "Want to join us?" She looks at me. "How about you, Emma? You in for a movie?"

I shake my head. Olivia's parents drive her crazy and they aren't around that much but they're here, truly here, even if it's not the way Olivia wishes they were, and I'm like a kid with her face pressed against the window, all the things I want and can't have right in front of me.

I spy a family.

I miss Mom so much.

"I'm going to hang out with Emma," Olivia says. "She can spend the night, right?"

"Sure," Olivia's dad says. "Is it okay with Dan?"

I nod.

"Do you need anything?" Olivia's mom says, and I shake my head because what I need isn't something anyone can give me. She looks at Olivia, kisses the top of her head, and then leaves, turning to the beeping gadget in her hand. Her dad grabs a package of crackers and wanders out, eating them one-handed as he starts to look at the cube again.

Some people think Olivia's hatred of technology is an act, like she's pretending or whatever. But she really does hate it. It's not so much because of her parents—although I think that's part of it—as it's what she doesn't want her life to be. She thinks it's sad that people would rather talk without ever seeing each other.

"I just think life should be lived, you know?" she's said to me more than once. "And how can all the talking with a keyboard ever be like actually talking to someone? It can't. People need each other."

"I don't know," I always said. "I think it just makes life bigger. People are closer, actually."

"I'd rather have an actual talk with my mom instead of having her send me messages," she'd say. "Wouldn't you?"

"Sometimes," I'd say, and she'd say, "Okay, fine," but I get what she's saying now. Mom and I talked like everyone else does, in person and over the phone and in all the ways you can, but now that she's gone, I miss talking to her for real. Hearing her.

I could call her cell phone and hear her voice mail, but it wouldn't be her. I could send her an email and get back the "I'll be in soon!" message she put up before she left work, but it wouldn't be her either. I would just hear and see electronic ghosts, and I already have a live one to face every day.

I call Dan from Olivia's room.

"Hi," I say when he answers. "I'm spending the night at Olivia's. I'll come home in the morning to get a ride to school."

"I don't know," Dan says. "What about your homework? You left your bag in the car. Plus we still haven't talked about what happened—"

"There's nothing to say. You want a name. You pick it out."

"Emma, your mother would be so sad to hear you talk like this."

"She can't be sad though, can she?" I say. "She's dead. I'll see you in the morning."

And then I hang up.

He doesn't call back. I know he won't. I know that despite everything he says, he knows what he's done. That he saw Mom die and made his choice.

He saw her die, and he still went ahead and decided that the baby was worth more than Mom and how scared she'd been about the pregnancy. About dying.

And he didn't even ask me what I thought. Not about Mom. Not about the baby.

Not once.

He just decided the baby was worth everything.

10

I wake up in the middle of the night and I can't fall back to sleep because I remember the day Mom came home with the official news that she was pregnant. Dan was with her and he was smiling so hard I thought his face must hurt. I'd never seen anyone so happy.

Mom didn't look like Dan did, and when he ran up to the nursery to get the sketches he'd been doing, she sat down at the kitchen table.

"Hey," I said. "So what's it like to be knocked up?"

"Scary," she said, and then bit her lip. "I just…I'm not young like I was with you, Emma. It was easy then. I never thought about what could happen. How I might lose you."

"Where am I going?"

"You know what I mean," she said. "Being pregnant is risky. And it's really risky for me."

"Yeah, but you're disgustingly healthy. That clot didn't even slow you down even though you were supposed to rest. It's like when Dan and I got the flu. What did you get? Nothing. Not even a cough."

"You two were the worst," she said. "Couldn't even have a fever at the same time, but what can I say? I love you."

"What's that?" Dan said, coming into the room.

"The flu," Mom said. "Remember?"

"How could I forget?" Dan said. "Emma and I suffered, and you never even coughed."

"That's what I said!" I said and Dan grinned at me. I looked over at Mom. She was staring at the kitchen table, but she wasn't looking at it. It was like she was looking at something far away.

"Mom?"

"Hey," she said, blinking and looking at me. "I spy a family."

"Yeah, you do. Three, soon to be four." I grinned at her.

She blinked again. "I think I'd better go sit down. I don't want to take any chances."

"Oh honey," Dan said. "You're already sitting down."

"I mean somewhere...I just..." Mom trailed off.

"Everything's going to be fine," Dan said.

"Promise?" Mom said, and her voice was shaking a little.

"Promise," Dan said and kissed her.

I smiled and said, "You guys," like I always had, like I thought I always would and the thing is, Mom was scared.

She was scared and I didn't see it. Not like I should have. I just thought it was the idea of the baby or the fact that she was over forty or maybe even giving birth itself, which sure didn't sound like fun to me.

But now I think Mom *knew*. I think that somehow, she knew that something was going to happen to us. That something was going to break our family.

I grit my teeth and close my eyes. I don't want to think about this anymore.

I stare at Olivia's dark ceiling and remember Caleb Harrison looking at me. Asking me what my problem was, and then staring at me and Mom and her stomach and then Dan and me.

I think about what I saw in his eyes before I looked away.

Anger.

And, weirdly, understanding.

11

I get back to the house in the morning and find Dan sitting in the kitchen, hunched over a stack of papers. He's still there when I come back from showering and getting dressed.

"I need a ride," I say, looking at the muffins he's made, which are cooling on the counter. Chocolate chip, my favorite.

I ignore my stomach's rumbling.

Dan looks at me.

"Do you want a muffin?"

"No. I need a ride, like I said."

"I'd still pick you up after school even if you'd gone with Olivia," he says. "I know how much you want to see—"

"I'll be in the car," I say, cutting him off. Having Dan take me to school sucks, but I want him to remember that

I'm still here because after what happened to Mom, what's to stop him from deciding I'd be better off somewhere else? Maybe he really would ship me off to some boarding school or worse, Mom's parents. Not that I know they'd take me, which makes it even crappier.

Dan comes out in a few minutes, shuffle-walking like he's an old man.

"I need to tell you something," he says when we're on the road. "It's about your mother's hospital bills."

That stops my worry fast, fast, fast. "Let me guess. Someone else is paying them."

He blinks. "How did you know?"

"I saw the stack. How else could you?"

"I—well, I've been working, or trying to, but I'll never earn enough to pay for the house and everything plus your mother's care."

I look away from him, stare out the window. "Her *care?*"

"Yes," he says, and I rest my head against the glass because he sounds like he means it, he really does. He really thinks that what he's done is *caring.* "Luckily, some people have set up a fund. It's for the baby and your mother."

Something in his voice makes my stomach hurt, like it's being twisted around and then shoved up toward my throat. "And what do they want in return?"

"There's a court case in Florida. A woman just passed away. She was pregnant and her husband wants to try to save the baby, but her parents—"

"Let me guess, her husband wants you to talk to them," I say, cutting him off. "Or are you going to talk in court about what you've done?" I turn to stare at him, and Dan's cheeks blaze bright red.

"It's not that simple," he says slowly. "He wants the baby, and her parents—"

"Fine. You should go down there and cry and say how sorry you are about Mom, how much you loved her, and how you're only trying to keep your little boy alive. Throw in something about how you know Mom would be so proud of you, covering your pain to focus on the baby."

"I am in pain," he says, his voice cracking. "I loved her, and I'll love her forever. I understand that you don't want to hear this, but your mother wanted this baby, and I know she'd—"

"She's dead! You can't ask her what she thinks or how she feels and you never, ever did. You remember her being pregnant and happy. You don't remember how scared she was. You don't remember how things really were."

"I do, and—"

"She knew," I say. "She knew something was going to happen. You don't remember how she looked when she had to go on bed rest. You don't remember how she'd just sit in her chair at night and hold her stomach like she knew it was going to break her. But you know what? I do. And I get to see what broke her every day. I get to see it and you want it and you'll get it and I hope..."

I trail off because Dan has pulled over, stopped on the side of the road, and is staring at me, white-faced.

"You hope what?"

"I hope she forgives you," I say, but that's not what I was going to say and we both know it.

Dan blows out a breath and pulls back onto the road. His hands are shaking on the steering wheel. He doesn't say another word until we're at school.

"Your mother would be ashamed of you," he says quietly. "Be angry at me, Emma, but don't ever be angry at your bro—"

I get out of the car and slam the door shut on him. His words.

He's right, though. Mom would be shocked by what I almost said. By what I was thinking.

Mom was terrified of the pregnancy, but she loved Dan. She wanted to make him happy, and I know she would be sad to see how things are between us now. That she would tell me not to blame anyone, that things happen and choices are made.

She would tell me hate only destroys.

I know this because she did.

"Hate almost killed me after your father died," she told me once, when I was nine and decided I wanted to know everything about him. "I was so angry, Emma. Angry at your father for driving in the rain. Angry at him for not somehow knowing that there was going to be an accident. About a month afterward, I was sitting alone, just staring at nothing, and I was hit with this wave of..." She trailed off.

"I went to his books—I'd boxed them all up because I couldn't bear to see them," she said after a moment. "I opened a box and got one out. I sat down with it and just started ripping the pages out. If he'd seen me, he'd have been so horrified. But he couldn't. And I thought 'Good, that's what you get for leaving me.' I missed him so much, I loved him so much, and yet I hated him for being gone."

"You hated him?"

She nodded.

"Were you…were you sorry that you…?"

"Oh, no," Mom said. "Never. You were the best thing that ever happened to me. But even knowing that, I would look at you when you were little and know he'd never see all the things you were able to do. I knew that he'd want to be there. But he wasn't and I hated that and I hated him for it too, and the hate was so…it was like a pit, Emma. I couldn't ever see the bottom of it and I finally realized if I didn't stop, it would take over my whole life."

"You really hated him?"

Mom looked at me. "When someone you love…when they die, you want it undone. You'd do anything to have them back, and it's easy to believe that if only this had happened or that had happened, everything would be fine. And that's what makes you angry. What makes you hate. You don't want to believe that sometimes bad things happen just because they do."

"Mom, I'm sorry," I whisper now as I step into school, and I hope she hears me. That she forgives me. That she can help me find a way to untangle the knot of hate in my heart, because it's there.

It's there, and I feel it.

It's there, and I can't make it go away. I understand what she meant now about the edge and how hate can take over everything. I see it. I feel it.

But I don't know how to stop it.

And the one person who could, the one person who'd be able to pull me back, is gone.

12

I'm in a pretty bad mood when Olivia finds me, and she takes one look at my face and wordlessly hands me a rubber band. Olivia's mom is a worrier who had a pretty messed-up childhood, and she always wears a rubber band around one wrist so that when she feels a burst of worry or a bad memory coming on, she can snap it against her skin and remind herself that she's here.

I put the rubber band on and give it a good yank. It stings—a lot—but I don't feel better. I already know I'm here. I already know what's on my mind.

Anger.

I'm starting to get scared at how angry I am, though. At how, when I try to find a way out, even for a second, I can't.

I snap the rubber band again as Olivia opens her locker. Still nothing. I do it again, and again, and then the band breaks, falls off my wrist and to the floor.

I stare at it. Someone steps right on it, and then it's gone, trampled off down the hall.

I look at my wrist. There's a red welt on it.

My mother has marks on her skin from the tubes and needles. She has to be turned and moved so her skin won't get sores.

"Okay, that clearly didn't work," Olivia says, grabbing my arm as she closes her locker door. "Come on, we gotta get you to your locker before classes start."

"I left my books in Dan's car," I say, and look around as Olivia says something about finding a notebook for me to take to class.

I see people walking by. Fast, slow, laughing, frowning. So normal. I hate that too.

And then I see Caleb Harrison standing by a locker, staring at me. I see him look at my wrist, at my face, and I can't see anyone walking by anymore.

He saw me yesterday. He saw me with Mom yesterday.

He knows something's wrong with me.

"Here," Olivia says, sticking a notebook into my hands just as the bell rings. "See you later."

I nod. What happened to Mom isn't a secret, but the whole baby thing never really got much attention. I thought it would—I thought it would pull in the nighttime reporters, the ones who are seen on TV everywhere—but it didn't. There were a couple of things locally, sandwiched in between stories about allegations surrounding the governor, but that was it.

"Death...and life," they always said, like my mother and what happened to her could be boiled down into three words and a pause.

Some people in my classes said they were sorry or asked how I felt, but that was right after it happened, and when I didn't break down and scream, when I kept coming to school, things went back to how they'd always been. Who was applying where, who needed what SAT score, who was going to hire someone to help them write their entrance essay and who was stressing out and how badly it would screw their grades.

On the news, there were murders and robberies and local sports heroes and possible rain showers.

That was it.

Mom got five days. Five days in the local news. Five days when people talked about her. When they noticed she was gone, when they asked questions, but those days passed. It was enough time for them but not for me, and it still isn't. The thirty-day mark since she died looms in front of me because if she makes it till then, if she stays dead but her body is still alive, chances are her body will hold out long enough for the baby to—I can't think about this, not now. I don't want to think about it at all. I don't want to think about anything.

Except, as I head to class I wonder why Caleb Harrison was staring at me.

What he sees that no one else seems to.

13

"You haven't turned in your New Deal paper," Anthony says to me in second period, just before the teacher starts talking.

I shrug. A month ago, Anthony would have been telling me his paper was longer or had more sources. Six months ago, he would have said the same thing and I would have said, "And we'll see who gets the better grade, won't we?" and he would have responded, "Emma, your competitive streak worries me," and I'd have said, "I know it does," and think we were flirting.

That's really what I thought. I thought Anthony—so determined to get into the right school, to be king of everything—was the guy. The boyfriend who could be mine if only I could get him to notice me.

I was wrong, but I didn't know that until after I'd made the disastrous mistake of hooking up with him.

It was four months ago, I think. I used to know it to the day, even to the hour, but I don't now.

We'd been working on a project for Advanced Chemistry together, doing an experiment on chemical compounds and reactions at night, just me and him with our chemistry teacher down the hall in his office snoring so loudly we could hear him.

So there we were, writing about chemical reactions, talking about them, and Anthony said, "I hope you realize I'm still going to get the best grade."

"I realize you think you will."

"I like your conviction," he said. "That's not supposed to be a seven, by the way."

"It isn't a seven, it's a one. I guess I can't say I like your ability to read handwriting."

"I have other qualities," he said.

"Please," I said, and felt so….well, this is humiliating, but I felt so flirty. Sexy, even. Like everything around us was charged.

"You've got moxie," Anthony said, and only he could say something like that with a totally straight face.

"Well, jeepers," I said, and he grinned.

"You're lovely."

Lovely. No one had ever called me lovely. My mother said I was cute, which everyone knows is mother code for "you look like a regular girl, sweetie," which is fine except regular is boring, regular gets you to seventeen without any boyfriends and a few nothing kisses at various parties.

"Lovely?" I said.

"Everything about you is lovely," he said and I—though I wish I hadn't now—kissed him. Just like in the movies, I moved in and kissed him and he kissed me back and the experiment got ruined but I got felt up on a lab table and went home with the memory of Anthony saying, "Well, I can't say I regret this outcome" as he tucked in his shirt. I practically floated all the way there.

The next day, he acted like nothing had happened. When I first saw him, he was talking to a bunch of people about the need to promote student government awareness (the popular people won the elections, but Anthony was always treasurer and was always convinced everyone cared as much about how much money the yearbook got as he did) and he waved at me. Like he did to everyone else who walked by.

"He's distracted," Olivia said. She'd heard what had happened, of course, and after a millisecond of silence had said, "Wow! That's...Anthony! And you! Anthony and you!"

Except it wasn't. In English, when we got our latest papers back, he said, "Look at this," and then motioned for me to show him mine.

I wanted more than grade comparing. I wanted kissing. I wanted talking, and not just about who had the better grade. I wanted into his heart.

Still, he acted like nothing had happened.

I cried and I talked to Olivia. I told Mom, and she said, "If he's acting like a jerk, he probably is one," and I told her I was telling things wrong, that it wasn't like that.

She said, "Emma," like only she could, with so much love in those four letters, and that was it.

After three days, I finally worked up the nerve to talk to him. I did it at the end of the day, went over to his locker after most everyone had left and he was talking to two freshmen, telling them that extracurriculars were important, but that they had to be the right ones.

"Anyone can sign up for drama," he said. "Debate, now, that's different. That's an art form, and one colleges love. Do you like discussing issues?"

"I don't know," one of the freshmen said and Anthony said, "See, debate helps with that. You'll know things. You'll be able to talk about anything. Trust me."

"I mean, I don't know about public speaking," the freshman said and Anthony said, "Well then, why would you want to sign up for drama? That's public speaking."

The freshman said, "No, I mean…" and then trailed off as Anthony said, "Look, you clearly need to think about it. It's your future, though."

He turned to me after they left and said, "Emma, what brings you by? Worried about the new assignment in history? I think you'll do fine."

"No," I said. "I—the other night."

"Oh," he said. "I don't really need the extra credit now, but I can come in and help you if you can reschedule. I just can't make it on Thursday nights anymore because I'm starting to volunteer to deliver meals to old people. Did you know mileage for that is tax-deductible? Or would be, if I paid taxes."

"Right," I said, as my joy, which had already shrunk considerably, shriveled into nothing. "You do remember that we made out, right? And you said I was…you said I was lovely."

"Of course," he said, smiling at me. "It was a very memorable moment and you *are* lovely. You know I adore you, Emma. I mean, you must know that. You're intelligent enough, after all."

"You—" I said, but coming right on the heels of the declaring, he'd turned back to his locker and was grabbing his bag like everything was over, said and done.

"You adore me?" I said, and he shut his locker, put an arm around me and said, "Of course. What's not to like? You're sweet and you're quite smart. How could you not have a place in my heart? Plus you find me attractive, which is always a nice thing to know."

"I—"

"I can tell I've upset you. Will you walk with me?"

I did, and he said, "I'm focused on college," as we stepped down the hall. Our footsteps were perfectly in sync. "And being with someone—well, at our age, can we really understand what a true relationship is? Do you feel you understand it? I know I don't."

I'd heard Anthony say lots of things. Interesting things. Smart things. Some stupid things.

But never this kind of crap, and I stopped walking.

"I understand you said I was lovely so I'd let you feel me up," I said, and he stopped too and blinked at me.

"You're angry."

"Yes," I said, and then, oh, then my voice cracked and I said, "I thought we—I thought what happened meant something."

"It does," he said, taking my hand, walking again and I walked too, watching my hand in his as he talked. "It did, and it does. But one moment doesn't mean everything. It can't. If it did, we'd be letting one act define who we are and you're bigger than that. I'm bigger than that. We both want the same things, Emma. We can talk about this more if you want, as I've always found the connection people make between physical action and emotion fascinating."

We were outside and I looked at him, at this guy I'd let shove his hands inside my shirt, and realized he believed everything he said and what had happened between us was...

Nothing.

I pulled my hand free of his and said, "See you later, Anthony."

I was proud of that, of how I just pulled away and walked off.

I didn't cry until I got to Olivia's house.

"One moment, my ass," Olivia said after I'd told her everything. "Who else would ever even go near him? He should be kissing your feet and thanking you for touching his funky self."

"If that's true, then why did he blow me off?"

"Because he's an ass. And he's a—what do you call it? Obsessed with yourself."

"He's not a narcissist," I muttered, sniffling, and then dragged myself home, heart battered and self-confidence shot. I'd really thought he liked me, but it turned out he liked someone else more.

Himself.

Olivia was right. Anthony was—and is—a narcissist, and as time passed I saw it. All of what I thought was banter was really him worrying that I had better grades. All of him offering to help out and acting like someone out of a really old movie and speaking like it was 1850 was his way of reminding himself and everyone else that he was special.

And the making out happened because Anthony was just a guy and I'd launched myself at him. Why would he turn that down? He was, after all, him, and to Anthony, he was pretty amazing.

"So, your paper?" he says again to me now, and I look at him.

"You win," I say. "You're the king of grades, the prince of GPAdom, the duke of whatever. Valedictoriandriandom, let's say."

"If you ever want to talk," he says, getting a handkerchief—of course he would have one—"you know I'm here."

I take the hankie. "What should we talk about?" I look at him and I know he sees my haunted eyes. My empty, furious smile.

I know he sees that I don't give a crap about my grades, about school, about all the stuff that used to matter so much to me.

He blinks at me, opens his mouth, then closes it. I hand the hankie back.

He doesn't say another word to me.

I look at him and try to remember that person I was not so long ago, but she seems so far away. She seems gone.

14

Caleb Harrison stares at me again at lunch.

I don't see him at first. I'm sitting with Olivia, picking at the fried rice in front of me, which is basically rice and limp broccoli, and then I…I don't know.

I feel it. Him.

I look up and there, across the cafeteria, in a corner by himself, is Caleb Harrison. And he's looking at me.

I elbow Olivia who says, "Oof!" and then follows my eyes.

"Wait, you said nothing happened yesterday."

"Nothing did."

"But he's—oh, never mind. He's looking out the window now. Remember how popular he was in middle school? And then he was all freaky drug guy and then stealing cars guy and now he's really screwed-up loner guy who puts cars into lakes. Scary."

No, I think. *Sad.*

Caleb Harrison is sad.

I don't know why he is, or how I know it. I just do.

I look at him.

He's looking at me again and I feel it, actually feel him looking at me, like from all the way across the cafeteria he's somehow able to see into me. That there's something in me he wants to see.

I take a sip of my soda and he's watching. I am hyperaware of it, of him, of how I suck a drop that's clung to my lower lip off, pulling it into my mouth for a moment and how I open my lips a little to breathe, because it's strangely airless in here and I want to ask him why but when I picture that, my walking up to him and saying, "Yeah, hi, I think you have a problem," he's standing up too and moving in, so close his hair brushes my face, so close his mouth is right next to mine and we're touching without saying a word, just standing there, close enough to kiss with his hands cupped around my waist, one sliding up, the other down and my hands are doing the same and he's breathing into me and I'm breathing into him and—

"Hey," Olivia says, waving a hand in front of my face. "Bell rang. What are you doing?"

"Nothing." At least, that's what I wish I'd been doing. Thinking.

"Your face is red."

"It's hot in here." He's gone now. Thank goodness.

"Not really. You sure you're okay?"

I nod and get up. I tell her that I'm fine. I go to class. I meet Dan after school. I go to the hospital.

I am not okay. I am not thinking about just Mom, like I have been for days, weeks.

I am thinking about something else. Someone else. Someone I don't even know and I pictured—

"Are you all right?" Dan says as we're heading to where Mom is. "Your face is a little red."

"It's from all the sex I'm having at school instead of going to class. It's tiring, but way more fun than trying to conjugate the past perfect tense of 'I see my dead mother every day.'"

"Emma!" Dan looks shocked and a little scared.

"Oh, relax. I won't do it in your bed when you're in Florida ruining someone else's life. When is that, by the way? I'll need to stock up on condoms."

"I've been worried and now I'm really concerned. I think you need help."

"Really? Well, talk it over with Mom and see how she feels about it. Oh, wait, she can't talk. You were concerned about her too, right? So maybe you can see why I'm not all that interested in your so-called concern."

"Emma," he says, sputters really, but I ignore him and head into the waiting room.

Where Caleb Harrison is standing with a magazine cart, having just heard everything I said.

15

Caleb sits down when I come in, sprawls on a chair with the cart in front of him, moving it back and forth with his feet. He doesn't look at me but then he doesn't need to, does he?

We both know what he just heard.

I know my face is red—it's so hot I can feel it—and I brace for another stare or a snarl like yesterday or something even worse, something crude that will make me feel just as bad as Dan sounded. (And looked too, but I don't trust Dan anymore. I wish I'd never trusted him.)

"Your mom's dead, right?" is what he says instead and it's so not what I expected and so blunt, so not covered in all the softness of *I'm sorry* and *terrible to hear* that now I just stare at him.

"I couldn't really tell yesterday," he says. "But that's what I figured. I remember hearing something about it. About how there's a ba—"

"She's dead," I say before he can finish his sentence. "But she's pregnant. So they're keeping her breathing and feeding her and everything else until she's twenty-five weeks along."

"They can do that? I mean, if she's dead—"

"Yes," I say, the word bitten off, sour and angry. "My step-father wanted…it's what he wants. So it's happened. You can be brain-dead and kept alive on machines. It just doesn't usually happen when there's…there's no hope for her."

He pushes the cart with his foot again. I find looking at it easier than looking at him, but when I dare a glance he's looking at the floor.

"How many weeks is she now?" he says after a moment where the only noise is the cart squeaking.

I swallow. "Almost sixteen." A little past twelve that final morning, the morning she went to get toast and fell down and didn't get back up. A little past twelve weeks pregnant the morning she died and that was it, should have been it except it wasn't, isn't.

"So she'll just…" He trails off. The cart squeaks again. He's frowning, but not like he's angry. Like he's thinking.

If he's thinking about my mother—just my mother—that would make, as far as I can tell, two of us who do that. Who've really done that.

"Yeah," I say, my voice tight. "If she makes it to thirty days the way she is now she'll just lie there, dead, for another ten weeks. Then Dan gets what he wants."

"Dan?"

"The guy in the hall. My stepfather."

"Oh," he says, and pushes the cart again. "That's pretty screwed up."

I sit down then, not facing him but not turned away either. High school teaches you lots of stuff, but one of the most important things is that you don't ever act like what someone's said has gotten to you, even if it has.

That's pretty screwed up.

Yeah, it is. It really is, and I know Olivia gets it, and I love her for it, but no one else has said it. No one. *Sorry* is all apologies but it isn't what this is about. No one's said the truth, the raw wound of what happened. What is happening.

Not until now, when I'm sitting here with Caleb Harrison who takes drugs and steals cars and who gets that what's happened to the family I used to have has exploded into something huge and very, very screwed up.

I miss Mom all over again then, wish she was here, that I could know I'd be able to walk into the house and it would be home. That I'd see her. The real her. I'd see her smile, push her hair back. Rub her forehead if she's had a bad day and asks for an aspirin, kicking her shoes off. She'd always ask what was for dinner, kissing my forehead before she'd turn to Dan and say, "Well, Chef, what's on tap?"

"You don't talk much," Caleb says.

I look at him, and I see that understanding in his eyes again. I don't get it, and I don't know if I like it. It's scarier than pity or Dan's beseeching stares. Pity I get. Dan wanting me to want what he does—it's Dan, so I get that too. But what do Caleb Harrison and I have in common? What could he understand about this? His parents are both alive and apparently dedicated to keeping him out of jail in spite of everything he does.

If there's one thing I learned from Anthony, it's the power of questions. I swallow, and hope my face isn't still as red as I'm afraid it is. "Why were you staring at me today?"

"Because I saw you with your mom yesterday." A magazine starts to fall off the cart and he reaches up, pushes it back in place. "Do you miss her?"

I look at the ceiling. My eyes are burning. I wish I knew how to make things better. Or even bearable. I'd settle for that. For just being able to breathe without feeling like it hurts.

"I get that. Missing someone, I mean," Caleb says, his voice quiet.

He *knows* and now I don't get it, I don't get it at all, and when I look at him I can't see how he understands. I just see him, so blond and pretty, so safe from everything he does because he has his parents. He has them doing everything for him.

"Oh, so you know what it's like to have a dead mother being kept alive so her so-called husband can get what he wants more than anything else?"

"No, but I know what it's like to live with a dead person."

"Your parents are both still…" I say and trail off as I remember that there is a dead person in Caleb's life.

His sister.

And then we just look at each other and I don't care that he's screwed up and gorgeous. I care that someone really does get what's going on. Sees it.

And I think he feels the same. Although I don't fall into the gorgeous category.

"I—" I say, and then Dan comes in and looks at Caleb, then at me. "Emma, you can go in now."

I get up, glancing at Caleb.

Dan sees it. "I'll just talk to your friend...." he says and Caleb snorts, gets up and pulls the magazine cart past both of us, out into the hall.

"Who is he?" Dan says. "I'm not sure how to ask this, but—?"

"Then don't, because even if there was something to tell, I wouldn't want to say it to you."

He looks at me, hurt all over his face, and I wish I could believe in it. In him.

But I don't, and I go see Mom. I sit with her. I hold her hand.

It's not enough today. I don't just want to sit here with her hand lying still in mine. I wish I could curl up next to her. That I could lie with my head on her shoulder. But I can't because she's in a hospital bed and it's filled with taped tubes and wires and IVs.

It's filled with her stomach, with what's in it, and when I look at her face I can't see her, I just see the tubes going into her mouth and down her throat and up her nose and that's all she is now. That's what she is.

"Mom," I whisper, and pull away, wrap my arms around myself. I can't talk to her. I can't tell stories about school, about anything. I can't pretend that life is normal except for this. Not now. Not today. I can't find her under what's in front of me.

I can't see anything of Mom. I just see a dead woman.

I pinch the bridge of my nose, hard, over and over until I know I won't cry.

When Dan comes to get me he tries to put a hand on my shoulder. I move away from it, from him.

"Emma, please," he says, his voice breaking, and I stare at him. He flinches and I know it's from the hate in my eyes.

He turns to Mom and I walk out, leave the hospital and go wait by the car. I see an ambulance come in, sirens wailing, before Dan comes out and gets in the car. I wonder what will happen to the person inside. I hope they are all right.

I don't see Caleb. I'm not exactly looking for him, but I am thinking about him. About what he said, about living with a dead person.

16

During the ride home, I think about Caleb.

I think about his sister, Minnie.

She died three years ago, when Caleb and I were both four-teen. She was seven, I think, or maybe only six. I know she was riding her bicycle and fell off.

That was it. That was how she died. That simply. There she was, on her bike, and then she was gone. Like getting up and going to get toast. Just a moment and then…gone.

I guess, now that I think about it, that's when Caleb started doing drugs. He must have really loved his little sister. Maybe everything Caleb's done is how he gets through it.

What would it be like, to live with that loss for three years? I can barely stand it, and it's been less than a month. How could anything be left inside you at all?

"Emma," Dan says, and I notice the car's stopped, that we're outside the house. I get out before he can say anything else, head up to my room and lock the door.

He knocks, but I pretend not to hear him. It gets easier every day. I go over to the window and open it.

I know eventually Olivia will come in.

17

She does, a while later, and frowns as soon as she sees me.

"What happened?"

"The usual."

"Uh-huh. You saw Caleb, didn't you?"

"Yeah."

"Did he say something?"

I shrug.

"Emma!"

"Not really. Sort of."

"Sort of? Like he sort of spoke? Or he sort of said something that upset you?"

"No, he didn't—I just saw him again and he knew about Mom. He did see me with her yesterday."

"Oh." Even Olivia hasn't seen that. "What did he say?"

"That it was screwed up."

"Emma—"

I shake my head. "Do you remember his sister?"

"His—oh, yeah," Olivia says. "Minnie. Fell off her bike and didn't have her helmet on, right? My parents were all, 'That's why we made you wear a helmet, Olivia.'" She shakes her head. "Remember how awful it was? I wanted a pink one, like yours, and had that weird-shaped silver one."

I nod, and she shakes her head. "Parents." She blushes, looks at me. "Sorry."

"Don't. You can't be weird on me. For real, not now, okay?"

"It was bad today, wasn't it?"

"Yeah," I say and she hugs me and says, "I'm sorry. I'm so sorry," and I cry like I always seem to be doing. I cry and when I'm done my eyes hurt and I have a headache and nothing's changed. You'd think I'd have learned that by now, that tears don't change anything.

You'd think I'd have run out of them.

But I haven't.

18

Mom did it. Well, she didn't. Her body did it, because today is day thirty.

Thirty days of Mom being dead but kept alive and at the start of week sixteen it was okay, it was in the distance.

That distance is closed today.

I have missed school or a weekend or maybe both. I don't know. It doesn't matter.

Olivia came by a few times, but aside from, "Emma, eat. EAT," I can't remember another thing she's said. I've just felt empty inside, silent, and the one time Dan knocked on my door and said, "Emma?" I said, "Do you miss her at all?" and listened to the drone of his voice, words buzzing over me.

I know I can't stay in my room forever. The thing about Mom dying is that the world didn't stop. It didn't even slow down. It's flowers and cards and everyone understands but no one does because Mom wasn't Mom to them. Without her it's like I'm living inside a mirror. I see things, I do things, but they are just surfaces and nothing more.

I'm numb, so numb, because thirty days is here but when I'm in the shower staring at the water, I wonder if Caleb feels like that about Minnie. Is loss this constant pain, not mental, but actual pain? It's like even my teeth hurt, but there's a fog over it, one that makes the pain hurt and yet leaves me carved out too.

Is grief this forever wishing for what was even though I know I shouldn't?

I shake my head, water splashing everywhere.

Mom loved to take baths. She actually took one the night before she died. I sat on the floor next to her tub, smelling the "calming" bath beads, oily bubbles, she'd put in. She'd put her hair up, stuck it in a half-knot that was already falling down and pushed the bubbles around as we sat there.

"You don't have to start on that paper now," she said. "You can relax. Watch some TV. Hang out with your old pregnant mother."

"But—"

"You don't have to try so hard," she said, reaching one hand out and touching mine, her skin hot and slick. "I love you no matter what."

"I know," I said and she squeezed my hand.

"So then let yourself breathe once in a while. Smell the roses. Go for it. Other inspiring things I can't remember now and so on." She grinned at me. "You do know what I mean, right?"

"Dan's going to come up and make you get out of the tub soon."

"You two." She sighed. "Am I allowed to brush my hair?"

"I don't know. Dan's got the pregnancy book. I'm going to read it after I get half of my New Deal paper done."

"Don't work on it tonight, okay? Watch *Covert Ops* with me."

I didn't. I worked on my homework and started pulling together ideas for my paper, blew a kiss at Mom when she stuck her head in and said, "Okay, I guess that's a no on the TV. Don't stay up too late."

"I won't," I said, half glancing at her as I read about FDR and his plans.

Her hair was down and dry. The lamp in my room cast a shadow on her face.

That was the last time I ever saw her.

Thirty days ago today, and I turn off the shower and watch the water run down the drain, circling, circling until it's gone.

I get dressed, putting on clothes from the pile scattered around my bed. I realize, for the first time, that the rest of my room is boxed off to me. I could pick up the books piled on my desk. The earrings on my dresser I'd bought shopping with Mom the week before she took that last bath.

But I can't.

I unlock my door, the reminder of putting in the lock—of Mom—almost bringing me to my knees and then I go downstairs.

It's early—I woke up before the sun rose and watched it come up, light tearing up the dark, and just thought *thirty thirty thirty thirty.* Thirty days. Mom's gone but still here and that's how it will be for another—

I can't. I just can't think it. I walk into the kitchen and Dan is there, looking like he hasn't slept. He's reading a book and I see it's the pregnancy book, the one he was reading the night before Mom died. The one I was going to read.

He sees me and puts the book down, pages up so I can't see the cover, the serene portrait of a woman holding her belly. A woman, alive.

"Do you want some breakfast?" he says. "I could make something."

"It's thirty days today," I say and he nods, his eyes filling with tears. I wish I could take all of my own back now. I don't want to be anything like Dan.

"I thought that might be you—well, why you were in your room," he says. "I asked one of the doctors at the hospital about it. She says she'd like to meet you. Talk to you. She thought it was interesting that you didn't come with me to see your mother during this period."

Interesting? *Really?* All because I sat in my room and thought about her. The real her, not the one I have to see.

Not that one who breaks me over and over again.

"I'd like a waffle," I say, and Dan looks at me, surprised, and then smiles, huge, bright, and gets up, moving around the kitchen. He gets out bowls and boxes, eggs and spoons, and plugs in the waffle iron I bought for him two Christmases ago.

"Here," he says a few minutes later and I look up from the

table—where did Mom touch it before she fell? I've never asked. Was it here? Over there? Did she not touch it at all, just walk straight to the toaster? Was Dan looking when she fell?

When did he know what he would do? After the ambulance came? After the doctor said she was gone?

Or did he know all along? Deep in his heart, had he made his choice the moment two years of drugs and testing and waiting brought Mom home to tell him what he so longed to hear?

He puts a waffle on the table. I hold on to the chair in front of me. I smell flour and eggs and milk and chocolate, which Dan always puts in waffles for me.

Mom would say, "Dan, you shouldn't spoil her," and Dan would say, "Chocolate isn't spoiling. Love isn't spoiling."

"You went shopping."

He nods. "We didn't have much to eat."

No, we didn't. Food goes bad. It spoils.

I swallow.

"I'm not hungry."

"But you said—Emma, I can hear your stomach!"

Dan is standing with his hands pressed together like he's praying and in the silence of the kitchen I hear a slight gurgle, a churning. It is my stomach, awake and moving.

Inside my dead mother there is a baby. It needs to eat. I suppose it has a stomach. I don't know. I don't want to think about it.

Thirty thirty thirty thirty.

"I'm going to the car," I say.

"You have to stop this," Dan says. "She wouldn't want you to punish yourself like this. It's not your fault that she died."

"I know it's not my fault. Are you going to take me to school?"

"Emma, I lost her too. We both lost her. I miss—"

I leave then. I walk outside, past the car and down the driveway. I cannot be here. I cannot see him, not now. I can't say anything else and I'm afraid that if I do he will find a way to make it so I can't see her. That he will—he could do anything to me because he's my guardian now. He could even have me committed.

I feel sick.

Mom wanted him to be my guardian. I wanted him to be my guardian too.

We both thought he was good at taking care of things.

And then she died.

I hear the car, hear Dan. "Emma, get in."

I look at the car. "Are you going to send me away?"

"What?" There's silence for a moment and then he sighs, a battered sound, and then I hear the horn beep over and over, the sound muffled, start-stop-start-stop.

I look over and see he is hitting it. Dan is smacking his hands into the horn, face red, wet with tears.

He stops. "I would never send you away," he says. "You're my family."

Thirty thirty thirty thirty.

I don't believe him, but I want to be here. I have to be here. Mom doesn't need me like I want her to, but I am all she has.

I get in the car.

"Emma, please know I wanted your mother and you, I wanted *our* family. That hasn't changed a bit. I wish that we were all—"

"Yes," I say so he won't say anything more. He does, he's wishing and wishing, but I don't listen.

I don't believe in wishes anymore.

19

Caleb isn't in school. I notice before first period and again at lunch. I don't say anything to Olivia, who saw Roger at the mall on Saturday and tells me all about it. I listen to her story of a fast-beating heart and flushed face and hesitant conversation like I am an old woman.

Heartbeat. That's what's keeping Mom here. I try to not think about it, but I can't because she doesn't have one.

Heartbeat. It's just a word. A word.

It's more than that.

"Hey," Olivia says, waving a hand in front of my face. "You're just sitting there nodding," she says. "This is really huge for me. He said it was great to see me. Not good, not fun. Great." She starts to say something else but then stops and says, "What's going on?"

"It's been thirty days since she died," I mutter.

"Thirty...oh," Olivia says. "So then—"

"Yeah," I say. "The doctors said if she made it through thirty days, the odds were stronger that she'd make it long enough for them to—so that eventually they can go in and get the baby out." I wipe my stupid welling eyes. "I'm sorry. I know everything with Roger is huge, I do. Tell me again."

She shakes her head. "It sounded stupid when I was saying it. Who cares if he said it was great to see me?"

"Great is better than good. Or fun."

"I could walk by his locker after lunch and see if he says anything." Olivia plays with a button on her shirt. "Should I? No, wait, I can't do that. What if he doesn't say anything?"

I look at her, the one person who I know loves me, and think about Mom in the bath that last night.

"I think you should go for it."

"Really?"

I nod.

We go and he's there and he says, "Hey, Olivia," and she says, "Hey," back and squeezes my hand so hard it hurts after we've walked away, but it's a good hurt. Her smile makes me smile and it gets me through the rest of the day and to the hospital, up to the floor where Mom lies.

To Caleb and his cart passing us in the hall on the way to her, to me sitting in a chair in the waiting room.

I realize I am waiting—hoping—to see him as I stand up and walk out into the hall. He's at the door as I get there, and we both stop and look at each other.

"I was waiting for you," I say, and immediately wish I

could take it back. It's true, but I shouldn't have just said it like that. Or at all.

"Oh," he says, and looks at the cart. "I—uh—" His hair falls in his face and whatever it was before, those moments where I looked at him and thought *he knows,* they seem far away now. He's just a guy standing there, made awkward by a strange girl with a round face that doesn't have the curves and grace of his.

"Not like that," I say, because it isn't like that, or even if it was (just a little—okay, a lot), I know it can't be. I know what goes together and it is not me and someone who steals cars and gets high. It's not me and someone who looks like him. It's not me and anyone like him.

"Not like what?"

"Like whatever is normal for you."

"Nothing is ever normal in any hospital," he says.

"You've been to more than one?"

"Five. Three for Minnie, two for me. Stomach pump and a dislocated shoulder, and every single hospital had the same color walls and the same awful lights. Not normal at all."

Thirty, I think, and swallow.

"You weren't in school," I say, to stop what I'm thinking. "Are you okay?"

He looks at me and then pushes his hair back with one hand. His eyes are wide and very green, even under the hospital lights. He looks so surprised.

"Emma?" Dan says, and it's time for me to go, to see Mom. I leave without looking back because I'm embarrassed and just…I don't know. I shouldn't have said anything to Caleb.

"Hi, Mom," I say when I'm sitting next to her. I don't say *thirty*. I don't say anything about that at all.

"Today was okay," I say instead, and tell her about Olivia and Roger. I look at her still face. I know there is nothing to see, that who she was is gone but she's here. She's still here, right here.

Except she isn't.

I should know this by now, but grief is slippery, a tangle of thorns that dig in so deep you don't know where they stop and you start. You don't know where you are.

I think of Caleb and how he looked when I asked where he was. So surprised, like no one would ever wonder where he was. How he was.

He has thorns too, and I wonder if he knows where his end and he begins.

20

I see Caleb before first period the next morning. I'm alone because Olivia is at the orthodontist making sure her braces-free teeth are still straight. She got her braces off before high school started but I know she's afraid that she'll end up with them again. Her father had them twice, and so did her mother.

I am at her locker, though, because she wanted me to grab one of her notebooks and give it to her later. I haven't picked up the notebook. I'm staring at a picture of me and Olivia from last summer, the two of us sitting in my backyard laughing at something I don't remember now.

Mom took the picture. I remember that.

"You missed the bell."

I blink and look over at Caleb. He's looking at the picture, and then he looks at me.

"That was taken before, right?" he says, and how can he tell?

"You're smiling," he says, like I've asked him.

I stare at him.

I stare at him because he's right. I can't remember the last time I smiled for real. I turn away, shut the locker on the picture, the me that was, and then glance at him. His head is bowed a little, all that blond hair falling over his face, part of the trifecta Olivia told me about.

I see it, him, but I see something else too. His hair is something for him to hide behind. My own bangs are down past my nose now and I haven't gotten them trimmed. I don't push them back. I let them swing forward, shadow my sight.

I'm hiding too.

"Aren't you going to first period?" I say.

He shrugs. "Study hall, so no. You?"

"I—" I have Advanced French, or the class you take before French Literature, where you read French novels in French. I have taken French since the sixth grade and done well, beyond well, but now I just sit in class, the words washing over me, familiar but faraway sounding, like the echo of a song you can't quite remember. "No."

He pushes his hair back with one hand then, those green eyes on me, and I think of the lake. Of how I'd heard he sat and watched the car sink. I am sure, suddenly, that he did. "Yesterday I had...there was court stuff. Judge follow-up."

"Oh." I think of thorns, of grief growing deep. Becoming you. "Do you miss her?"

He looks away, and doesn't say a word.

I know what that kind of silence means, and clear my throat. "So what happened?"

"To Min—?" he says, and then stops. "Wait. You mean to me, right?"

I nod.

He heads toward the gym, the far end of the school, and stops after a second, looking back at me.

I am walking toward him, and then I am walking with him.

"You've probably heard it already," he says. "Drugs, theft, suck camp, my dad's car, and now community service at the hospital."

"For your dad's car?"

He walks over to the vending machines. Our feet hit the floor at the same time with every step. I like the sound it makes. "Yeah."

I look at him. I want to ask about suck camp, which I'm guessing was the "tough love" place his parents sent him to, the one that brought him home all cleaned up (mostly) until now. Until his dad's car.

But it's his story to tell, and I know what it's like to have to live with one. How hard it can be to think about, much less talk about.

"You have a dollar?" I say and he grins—I see the flash of his teeth—and digs into his pockets, pulling one out.

"You like cotton candy?" I say and he nods, glancing at me. His hair has fallen into his face again.

I put the dollar into the machine and press the button.

"Me too," I say as it falls. When I pull the bag out, it's silver and light, with a pink puff picture on it.

He pulls out another dollar and puts it in the machine.

"I didn't mean—"

"I know," he says, and buys another bag. He pulls it open right away, sweet smell all around us, sugar and fake color.

"I remember you," I say slowly, and I do, bits of things half-buried. Elementary school, and the beginning of middle school; a boy with blond curls and a big smile and huge green eyes that looked like they had a bit of the sun in them, strange but somehow so pretty that you noticed them. "You talked a lot. You had—you were—"

"I had friends," he says, smiling a little.

I nod, opening my own bag. The cotton candy isn't sticky. It pulls apart in soft little clumps. "And you used to chase Amy Gray all over the playground."

He laughs. Amy is still pretty chaseable, only she's been caught by a six-foot-tall volleyball player, Monica, and has been since we were freshmen.

"You used to try to trade your sandwiches," he says and I'd forgotten that, how when I was little Mom always bought the wrong kind of bread, the kind of stuff you see old people pick up at the supermarket and sigh when it thuds into their carts. Dan had slowly managed to get it out of the house after he and Mom started dating and I remember hugging him the first time I ate a piece of toast that didn't weigh half a pound.

"What?" Caleb says, and I shake my head.

"I just—my mom used to get that bread, you know? And I'd forgotten how much I hated it and how she would never let me try something else until—" That had been Dan too. He'd said that I should at least be allowed to try another kind of bread for a week. "It can't hurt her, Lisa," he'd said. "There's enough stuff in that bread she's been eating to keep her heart and the rest of her healthy until she's eighty."

I swallow and hear the bag crumple in my hand.

"So what happened to you?" I say again, and Caleb tosses his empty bag at the trash can. It misses and lands on the ground.

"I killed my sister," he says.

21

"You—she fell off her bike," I say, startled by the flatness of his voice. The sureness. How can he think Minnie falling off her bike was his fault?

How can he think her death was his fault?

"I was with her. Watching her. I had to do that a lot. Minnie was—she didn't like any of the nannies we had."

"You had a nanny? But you were—" I break off, blushing.

"Yeah, I was too old," he says. "I hated it. And Minnie knew it so she hated them too and she had 'impulse problems.' You know how there's a moment when you think about something before you do it? Minnie never had that. She'd just...anyway. She wanted to go bike riding and the last nanny had quit so we went to the park. My parents were always on me and her to make sure she wore a helmet but she hated it and I didn't want to deal with trying to get her to wear it so I didn't even bother trying. We got to the park and I was bored out of my mind sitting there, watching her ride around. Pissed off, you know? And then there was a car and I saw her...she flew off the bicycle and landed on the sidewalk. Her bike went in the lake and she just—she just lay there. People were screaming and all I could do was look at her. If she'd had a helmet on, she'd have lived. Broken bones, sure. But she'd have lived."

I don't know what to say. I look down at my crumpled bag of cotton candy. I pick up one of the bits I pulled free. The first bite is what I remember—the pure, almost-crisp taste of sugar followed by a hint of bitter, like there's so much sweet my mouth can't process it all. It hurts, a little, to swallow. "If I skip second period, will I get detention?"

He nods.

"I can't get detention. The...you know. Seeing my mom. I guess you can't get it either. You have to be at the hospital or else you'll get in trouble, right? With the judge or whatever and your parents?"

"How come you haven't said anything about me killing Millie?" His voice is so quiet.

"Because you didn't. She was hit by a car. You couldn't have stopped that."

"If I'd made her wear her helmet..."

"She knew she was supposed to wear one. You can't take the blame for that."

"Maybe." He swallows. "My parents think I should."

"My mother thought having a baby would make my family

better," I say, and I hear how my voice is shaking, dig my fingers into my palms. "She was wrong. Parents can be wrong."

The bell rings then, and both of us jump a little. Both of us look at each other.

"See you, Emma," Caleb finally says, and then disappears down a hallway before I can say anything in reply.

I don't see him at the hospital that afternoon, and Dan spends a long time talking to the doctor. I whisper to Mom about the bread and how I'd forgotten about it.

"'I met—there's someone who understands," I say. I haven't talked to her about a guy since the Anthony nightmare.

"It's Caleb Harrison," I say, and everyone would have something to say about that. Even Dan tried to say something that first time.

But she doesn't reply. Her stomach doesn't even move.

When it's time to go, Dan drives back to the house quickly, silently, and doesn't say anything to me when we get there, just gets out and goes inside.

Bad news about the baby, I bet.

I thought I'd be happy about it, but I'm—

I'm not.

I'm not happy. I'm not sad. I'm just…here. Numb.

I go up to my room and open my window. There's a note taped to it, Olivia's scrawled *Emma* on the front.

And on my roof is Caleb.

22

"Caleb?" I say, like he's not sitting right there, like I can't see him sitting with his legs crossed, his hair blowing a little in the wind.

"Hey," he says. "I didn't see you at the hospital this afternoon. I got stuck working on another floor. And I…I heard you and Olivia talking about the whole roof thing a while ago. Not that I meant to or anything, but I—" He breaks off, and although the sun is setting, I swear Caleb Harrison, car thief, is blushing.

"Anyway," he says, "I just came over. I don't know why."

He *is* blushing. Who would have thought Caleb Harrison could blush?

I look at him, and then climb out onto the roof. I've been out here with Olivia, and it's not so different with Caleb. I sit down next to him and a strand of his hair blows across my face, making my skin prickle.

It might be a little different.

I open the note from Olivia. She has pink stationery with little dots on it that she uses for important messages, and there are matching envelopes too. Those only get used for very special messages.

This message is in one of those envelopes, and apparently she's with Roger, who asked her out when she was leaving school. They're going to watch TV at his house.

This is something, right? she's written, and then *Call me later!*

Call me later! is underlined three times and I know she must be happy and nervous because of how hard her pen has dug into the paper.

"So what's up with you getting letters on your window?" Caleb says as I'm putting the note away. "Nobody writes anymore."

"Olivia does. You know about her technology thing, right?"

"Yeah, she was in my English class last year. Brought in her typewriter when we were supposed to be looking up stuff on library computers and asked about encyclopedias. I thought Mrs. Grimwood would have a fit. Is it true she doesn't even talk on the phone?"

"No, she will, but it has to be a landline. You know, like a phone in a house or a store or something."

"And she writes letters."

"Yeah, but only for important stuff."

"Like what?"

"Can't tell you."

He grins at me and it's a wide, beautiful thing. My heart does this weird stutter-skip in my chest and Olivia really wasn't kidding about what he looks like.

"So, where were you at the hospital?" I say because it is the only thing I can think of, because the wind and his smile and today have left me feeling like everything inside me is visible and I don't know if I want to be seen.

"Fourth," he says. "Lots of people waiting for surgery. Foot and gallbladders, mostly. I don't even know what a gallbladder is."

"It helps with digestion, but you don't have to have one, especially if it gets infected. Or if you get gallstones."

"Oh," Caleb says, leaning forward a little and looking at the ground. His hair falls over his face again. "You really are smart. I mean, I knew you were because of all the classes you're in, but still."

"What good is knowing about a gallbladder? It's not—I spent so much time worrying about stuff like that, stuff that doesn't..." I look down at the ground now. In the dark, it's hard to see. "Stuff that doesn't matter."

"Everything matters," Caleb says, and I look at him. He's looking up at the sky now, at the clouds, dark against the night sky, and the tiny bits of starlight that shine through them. "Or at least that's what I was told at suck camp."

"That's the thing your parents sent you to?"

"Yeah, after school ended last year they shipped me off to The Helping Center. I spent the summer walking up hills

and camping—which sucked—and being told that everything matters."

He doesn't sound like he believes it. "Does it?"

He's silent for a moment and then leans back against my
roof, still looking up at the faint light of the stars. "No. If everything matters, then nothing can because it's all the same.
And if it's all the same, then nothing is ever special. And
shouldn't there be—aren't there—special things? People?"

"Yes," I say, looking up at the sky too and thinking of
Mom.

"Yeah, so that part of camp sucked too," he says with a
short, sad little laugh. He sits up. "Sorry. It's dumb."

"Why?"

He glances at me and even though I can't see him that
clearly I am sure I've somehow startled him again.

"Just because," he finally says. "I already know what I did
and what my parents think of me. But I guess they just wanted
to be sure I knew. That I accepted it."

"But Minnie didn't die because you—"

"I gotta go," he says, standing up, and I look at his back.

"You don't accept it, do you?" I say. "You know it isn't
true. That's why you stole your dad's car. Because you won't
do what they want. Won't be what they want."

He freezes, and then looks over his shoulder at me.

"I was angry," he finally says. "I've said I was sorry but that
isn't enough for them. It'll never be enough."

I stand up and walk over to him, sure-footed after years
of me and Olivia hanging out up here. "I told Dan not to
do what he's done. Mom wouldn't want it. He said I was too

upset to think straight and I didn't know what she wanted. He still says that. And I…" I swallow. "I loved him, you know? But he just wants the baby. And so now we're waiting, and I know he wants me to want what he does. But I can't. I won't."

Caleb turns around. He's a little taller than I am, tall enough that I have to look up to see him.

"It's lonely," he says, not a question at all, and when I nod, he hugs me.

And I stand there on my roof, in the dark, being held by Caleb Harrison. That's all he does. Olivia is around, always, and she's here for me, but she doesn't get it. Not like Caleb does.

In the dark, with his arms around me, I don't feel so empty.

23

I almost forget to call Olivia but remember as I'm brushing my teeth and getting ready for bed.

"Sorry," I say when she picks up the phone.

"For what?" She sounds really happy.

"I should have called earlier." I should have done it right after Caleb left but I didn't. I just sat on the roof for a while, thinking.

Thinking about him.

"I wasn't home earlier," she says, and then laughs. "Emma, he's so amazing! We ended up talking for hours. Did you know his middle name is Thomas? And he hates candy corn too! And he kisses—"

"Wait, wait, wait. Kisses?"

"Yep," she says, and I can hear her smile. "He kissed me! I

actually wished I could have gotten in touch with you right then—well, not right then, but right after—because wow! Amazing! It was the best night of my life."

"So, are you two together?"

"He wants to go out this weekend. I told him I'd think about it."

"Really?"

"No." She laughs. "I said 'Yes!' practically before he finished asking me. Was that dumb? It was dumb, wasn't it?"

"Did he take it back?"

"No."

"Then how dumb can it be?"

"It's just—I'm really happy and then I'm really nervous and then I'm happy and—you get it," she says. "I'm never going to be able to sleep tonight. Maybe I should do something about my hair."

"Olivia," I say. Olivia likes trying new stuff. Bright green eyeliner. Putting a tiny fake tattoo of a star near her mouth. Wearing fake eyelashes. But once in a while, she'll do something extreme, and it's always with her hair.

And she always regrets it. Last year, she decided she wanted bangs and cut them herself. The result was beyond bad and took months to grow out. And the year before that, she decided she wanted to have black streaks in her hair but ended up with black spots.

"Nothing like before," she says. "I was just thinking about curling it."

"With what?"

"You can buy stuff to make it curly."

"Like a curling iron, or stuff in a box that comes with a list of instructions?"

"Instructions."

"No way. Remember the black dye? You don't want something like that to happen again, do you?"

"No, but I want to look…I want him to see me and think 'Wow.'"

"Then don't put anything in your hair."

"It's straight."

"It's pretty and you're totally at the nervous end of things right now, right?"

"Maybe. I just—you know last year there was Pete, and it ended up being nothing and I like Roger so much more and—"

"Pete was a jerk. He was a total party boyfriend, super nice when he was drunk and wanted to get you alone but a troll the rest of the time."

She laughs. "He was a total party boyfriend. And jerk. Okay, you're right, I'm just nervous. Roger isn't Pete. Right?"

"Right."

"Okay, so I am going to be completely calm about this now. Or at least change the subject. How was the hospital?"

"The usual."

"The usual?"

"Well, Dan seemed a little upset on the way home, but— well, you know. He does his thing. I do mine. And we both wait."

"You didn't see Caleb at the hospital?"

"Nope."

"Something happened," she says. "I can tell."

"I talked to Caleb at school. So, what happened at the orthodontist?"

"My teeth are fine, but nice try. What did you talk about?"

"Cotton candy."

"You and Caleb Harrison talked about cotton candy? Was it like something he ate when he got high? Is he doing stuff again? You know even the hard-core, have-to-get-high-in-the-bathroom-before-class fiends don't talk to him anymore, right?"

"He wasn't high, Olivia."

"So you talked to him about cotton candy. Anything else?"

I think of him standing on my roof. Of the things he said about where he's been. What his parents thought he did.

Of how he knows what being alone is like.

"Yeah."

"Emma, look, that 'yeah' sounded like it was a lot. I think you need to come out with Roger and me on Friday. He knows a lot of great guys."

"Olivia, you can't take me along on your date and I don't need one anyway."

"Look, I know things are awful. I think of your mom all the time too," she whispers. "But I don't want you to forget about everything else, Emma. How about I talk to one of Roger's friends and see if he—"

"No. I can't think about guys like that now."

"But you're talking to Caleb Harrison."

"It's not...it's different."

"Okay," she says, and I really can't think about it, about dating and all the things Olivia is doing.

But I am thinking about Caleb. About how he is nothing like everyone says he is. About how I stood on the roof with him tonight and felt more at peace, more alive, than I have in ages.

24

Dan is downstairs in the kitchen in the morning, like always, only today he isn't cooking or eating. He's sitting at the kitchen table, looking at something.

Looking at a picture of Mom.

I see it. I can't not see it, and I stop when I do, frozen by Mom's face. Her smile.

It's not a pregnant picture or anything. Just a picture of her.

"Do you remember this?" Dan says.

"Yes," I say, because I do.

The photo is from her last birthday, when Dan and I surprised her with a dinner-and-gift-celebration. I made a banner that said Happy Birthday, and Remember to Thank Your Banner Maker, and when she saw it, she laughed so hard she cried. The picture is of her shaking her head, wiping her eyes with a huge smile on her face.

I watch him smooth a finger over Mom's face, gently brushing over her smile.

I want to touch the photo. I want to hold it, I want to look at Mom up close, see her as she was. But I don't want to ask Dan for it. I don't even want to think about him looking at it, or why he is.

So I just say, "I'm ready to go now," and start to head for the door.

Dan clears his throat. "She was happy, right?"

I stare at him. I want to hate him and part of me does. Part of me hates him so much I can hardly breathe because of it, but another part of me remembers the guy who came into her life, into our lives, and made things better.

"Yeah," I say. "She was."

He must hear the break in my voice, the stress on *was*, the anger and grief I can't hide and won't because Dan did this, Dan is why we are here, like this, right now.

He must hear it because he looks at me.

"You and I. What's happened?" he says. "I look at this picture and all I can think about is how things were. How I've lost you too. Emma, I miss—"

"I really need to get to school," I say to stop him from talking more.

"Will you at least tell me how to make it right?"

"You can't. It's too late."

"It's never too late."

"Yeah, it is," I say, thinking of Mom, of how there is no

chance for her, how there's never been a chance for her, and still she lies in that hospital because of him.

I walk outside and get into the car.

After a moment, Dan comes out. And yet another day begins.

"Do you want the photo?" he says when we get to school, and Dan knows me. He knows how much I love Mom and of course he saw what was written on my face when I saw it.

Of course he knows how much I miss her.

"No," I say, and get out of the car.

In school, I don't look for Olivia. I can't handle seeing anyone, even her. I just walk around, step one two three four through all the halls, and end up by the vending machines. There are people waiting in line to buy caffeinated water and juice, our school's "healthy" answer to soda.

There are people buying candy bars too—a couple of years ago, they put in fruit instead, but sales dropped so low the candy came back.

I see a few people I know from class, and I see them glance at me and then turn away. I'm like Sara Walton was two years ago, the girl who would and could and did until she had a nervous breakdown.

Sara and I both went from being the person to beat to being the story of how you could—can—screw up, and I used to think Sara should have been stronger, that she should have focused on what was important: on getting the right grades, on doing everything possible to get into the absolute best school.

Now I get how she felt. How you see everything you've done and think, *Why? Why bother? Why*— I feel the tears welling and dig around in my bag, find some change and hold it tightly in my fist, the coins digging into my palm.

There is no why. That's what Sara figured out, and that's what I know now.

Things just happen and sometimes you wake up one morning and go to school and your mother dies.

I buy a bag of cotton candy when I'm finally in front of the vending machine.

"Emma?"

"Hey, Olivia," I say, and slide the candy out and into my bag, move aside so the next person can get what they're waiting for.

"Where have you been?"

"Walking around."

"Around school? Why? Are you looking for Caleb?"

"Olivia, no. I'm just—this morning wasn't so great, okay? Dan had a picture of Mom and started talking about her and then said he felt like he'd lost me too, and I just couldn't handle it."

"Oh." The bell rings and she looks at me.

She looks at me and I see pity. I know she loves me, but she also feels sorry for me and I don't want that, not now.

"I gotta go to class," I say and smile at her before I walk off. I turn around at the end of the hall and see her watching me. I wave to show I'm okay, and she waves back and then disappears.

The halls empty fast and there I am. Here I am.

I am Emma, seventeen. I live with my stepfather. My mother is dead. Inside her is a baby.

I close my eyes. I do not want to think about this. Not about Mom or Dan's choice. Not any of it, but it is what I am—all I am—and how can I get away from myself?

I go outside. Just like that, I leave school. It's easier than I thought it would be. The part of me that tried so hard, that wanted all those A's and worked so hard—that part is truly gone.

But I've still never left school unless Mom—or Dan, after he and Mom got married—had to take me to the doctor or the dentist or I got sick. I've never just walked out. It seems so strange that you can do it.

But you can.

Outside it is quiet, the school a low hum behind me, voices from classrooms carrying, bleeding out through the walls, out into the air around me, but softly, softly.

It's sunny. I don't remember when I stopped noticing stuff like that.

I look up at the sky. There's the sun, bright and yellow. Clouds, white and fluffy.

It shouldn't be like this. The sun shouldn't be shining. There should be no weather, there should be nothing, but that's the worst thing about Mom dying. Nothing else stopped.

Only she did.

"What are you doing out here?"

Caleb. I look away from the sky and see him standing nearby, looking at me.

"I don't know. What are you doing out here?"

He runs a hand through his hair, sends it sprawling over his face. "I saw you come out and...I don't know. I guess I know the look on your face. I've just never seen it on someone else."

I look at what I can see of his face. "How does it look?"

"Bad."

I think of the people from my classes that I saw before, and how they looked at me and turned away. I think of Olivia and the pity in her eyes.

"It's all bullshit anyway," he says, gesturing back at the school, and then takes a step toward me, shoving his hands into his pockets. His hair parts enough that I can see his eyes.

He is looking at me, right at me. He sees me, and there is no pity in his eyes. He just *sees* me.

"You want to get out of here?" he says.

"Yeah," I say. "I do."

25

Caleb has a car, which surprises me. He sees my face and laughs, not at me but—well, it sounds like he's laughing at himself. And it's not a happy sound.

"By special permission," he says with a flourish. "My parents are too busy to drive me around, so I got to keep my license. It pays to be a lawyer who knows everyone around here."

Maybe I should be nervous about getting into a car with him, but I'm not. As weird as it might sound, I trust Caleb Harrison. He's not—who he was isn't who he is now.

I get that.

He drives us to the rich part of town, the part where all the houses are practically piled on top of each other, separated by slivers of immaculate lawn to pretend there is space.

They all look alike too, massive brick structures that stretch up and out and line streets with names like Park Avenue Lane.

He drives slowly, carefully, and I know which house is his the moment we turn onto Royal Crescent Court. It's huge—the largest house on the street—but it is also the loneliest-looking house I've seen besides the one Dan and I share. It's like the house itself knows something is missing. That someone is gone.

He pulls into the driveway, turns the car off, and then looks at me. "Inside is—there's stuff. My parents really loved Minnie."

I think of Dan, holding the picture this morning.

"Lots of photos?"

"Sort of," Caleb says, and his voice is strained.

He hesitates by the front door. I can't see his face through his hair and, on impulse, reach out to move it back a little. To see his face.

It's soft, not stiff with stuff like Anthony's or slick like Olivia's with the cream she rubs into hers every morning to make sure it doesn't frizz.

It's just hair, I know, but touching it sends a shock through me, a spark that makes my fingers tingle, sends my thoughts scattering, and when Caleb looks at me, I see he feels it too, whatever it is. I pull my hand away.

My fingers still tingle.

Then Caleb opens the door.

26

I have seen cemeteries. I should have seen one many times by now, over the past thirty-one days. I thought I would see Mom there, that I'd sit by a stone with her name carved on it and wish she was here.

Instead, everything went sideways, upside down, strange, and I have never ever seen anything like Caleb's house.

At first it looks ordinary. There are rooms. There is furniture. There are rugs. In the hall where we stand is a place to put umbrellas and a coatrack.

There is also a painting of Minnie. It hangs on a wall directly in front of us. It is as tall as I am, maybe taller. It is all that is on the wall.

Minnie, grinning, one hand raised like she's saying hello. Asking you to come closer.

There's more. In every room Caleb and I walk through—living room, dining room, kitchen, four other rooms that are filled with furniture but that I don't have a name for, there is Minnie. She is in little-girl things turned into art, a pair of sneakers resting on top of a table in a glass box, a set of barrettes mounted into a frame and put on an end table. She is in drawings, yellowed and curling at the edges all over the fridge, her name scrawled in the corner.

She is in paintings too. In every room, there is a painting. None as large as the first one, but they are the first thing your eye is drawn to. Among the furniture and the rugs and the things that make a room, a house, she is there, a girl in a picture, smiling.

She is blond and tiny, and behind her are grass and trees and bright, bright sky.

She is always smiling.

We stop in a room that I think is maybe another living room. A sitting room, maybe? A sofa and some chairs are placed by a fireplace with tiny pink ballet slippers on the mantel. A few photos sit on an end table. The windows look out onto what I guess is Caleb's backyard, a bit of grass and then a room of his neighbor's house. The curtains are green and match the rug. The sofa is soft-looking, the chairs wide.

It is like being inside a tomb. Everything about the room, the house, is about loss. It screams it without words. It scares me.

I reach out blindly and touch Caleb's arm. I move my hand down, touch it to his.

His fingers are cold and I look at him. He is staring at the portrait of Minnie and I see what people at school see when they look at me. I see why they turn away.

I see what grief does, how it strips you bare, shows you all the things you don't want to know. That loss doesn't end, that there isn't a moment where you are done, when you can neatly put it away and move on.

It never leaves you.

I look at the portrait. I don't remember Minnie that well, but I don't remember her as blond and tiny.

"I thought Minnie's hair was darker."

"It was," Caleb says, and his hand, in mine, is shaking a little. "And she was…my mother used to worry about her weight. She put Minnie on diets. The first one was when she was four. I remember that because Minnie cried. She didn't do that a lot. But she cried whenever Mom told her she was fat."

He looks at me. "But they wanted to remember her like she was…." His voice trails off, and I see he is looking at the end table. I walk over to it, his hand still in mine, and pick up one of the photos.

There are three people in it. The moment I see it, I can tell Caleb has his father's eyes and his mother's hair. They are standing together, smiling stiffly, and in front of them is a little girl—blond and tiny, just like the paintings —who is holding her arms out for someone. I see a hand reaching toward her, the edges of fingers, and one single blond curl.

"When she was little," he says, "she was beautiful. Everyone said so. People used to stop my parents and tell them how pretty Minnie was. Then she got older and people didn't say it."

He takes the photo out of my hand, moving away from me, our hands no longer joined, and puts it back down. "I wish…"

He falls silent and stays that way, looking at the photo.

I look at his back. At the way his shoulders are hunched.

I look at him.

"You're in it. The picture."

He looks over his shoulder at me.

"I was."

"Your parents took you out of it?"

"No, I did. My mother cried about not having any photos after the funeral, and I wanted her to have some. But we only ever took family photos on vacations. They didn't—there weren't any pictures of just Minnie."

"So you made some."

"Yeah," he says and turns away, looks back at the photo again. "I made some."

"Are there any of you?"

"No. I'm here. They have to look at me every day. That's more than enough for them."

I think of him taking his dad's car. Of how he watched it sink into the lake. The lake near where his sister died.

I think about what he said to me last night.

It's lonely.

He didn't just lose his sister. He lost everything. He's alone.

He's been alone for years and he's still here. He carries ghosts and blame that shouldn't be. He got twisted all around but never broke.

I walk over to him.

"Caleb," I say, and he looks at me.

I take his hand and lead him out of the room. Away from the pictures, the portraits, the pieces of Minnie's life lying around.

I don't know if I should take him out of the house or not. I can't believe he lives here, in this giant, furnished tomb. I can't believe I never wondered why he did the things he did, why I just accepted that he was a loser and never thought about it. About him.

"How do you do it?"

He's silent for a moment, looking at the floor, and then he looks at me.

"I don't know."

"You don't know?" My voice is shaky, cracking.

I want an answer. I want something to help me understand why Mom died and why she's still here. I want to know how to fix things. Caleb has survived loss. He lives with grief all around him, in him. He must know how he did it. How he does it.

He lets go of my hand. "I'm not—Emma, I drove my dad's car into the lake. I don't want to be in this house, I don't want this to be how things are. But I want a lot of things that can't happen, that won't happen, and that's what I know."

It's not what I want him to say, but it's the truth. I hear it in his voice. I know it in my heart.

Under the idea that we can all make our fates, that we have choices, is the reminder that sometimes we don't. That some-times life is bigger than our plans. Bigger than us.

"Okay," I say.

"Okay?" he says and I smile because he isn't okay and I'm

not okay, but what he's saying is okay. Is right. Sometimes you want things that can't happen. That won't happen. And it's just how things are.

"There need to be more words," I say. "Like a way to get that okay isn't possible, but it is okay."

"I don't think there can be a word for that. Do you...do you maybe want something to eat?"

I look around the hall, back toward the rooms we've just been in. This quiet, strange, sad monument to a girl that exists only in her parents' mind. "Here?"

"No. Well, sort of."

"Sort of?"

"Not in here," he says and looks back into the house too. "I don't—I've never brought anyone here before. You can see why, I guess."

"Yeah," I say, because I do, and we walk outside.

27

We eat lunch in his room.

His room isn't in the house.

It's above the garage, a small white room with a window that has no curtains. There are no rugs on the floor. No soft chairs. There is a bed, a small TV, a bathroom and, tucked into the corner, a tiny kitchen.

"The nannies used to live here," he says, going over to a small fridge. "And then my mom took a lot of pills after Minnie died. I started taking them too and then I found out if I took them and drank..." He looks over at me. "You know about this."

"I heard things."

"Right," he says, pulling out a pizza box and shutting the

fridge. "So there were pills and other stuff, and one night I lit my room on fire."

"On fire?" I hadn't heard about that.

He nods. "My mom was up—she doesn't sleep much—and she put it out. She, uh—when I woke up she was just staring at me. I started to say I was sorry and stuff and she just kept staring at me."

"She didn't say anything?"

He looks at the pizza box. "Not until I stopped talking. Then she said, 'Haven't you done enough?' I moved over here after that."

"Is that why you stopped…you know."

"What, getting high? You can say it. You can't get high just from saying the word." He blows out a breath. "Sorry. I…um…it's not why I stopped. The first car I stole, I—I hit someone. A guy. He had this little backpack with him. He was going to see his kid, who was at her first sleepover and had forgotten some stuff. I got out of the car and he was just lying there and that backpack was lying there and I thought he was dead. That I'd done what…"

He trails off and shifts so his hair falls forward, covering his face.

"The guy didn't die," he says after a moment. "I didn't believe it, even though he sat up after a second and started screaming at me about his leg and what I'd done. I can still see him right before he sat up and started yelling, you know? Minnie…" He shakes his head. "That's when I stopped. Why I stopped."

"You hit someone with a car?" I say, and I know he just

said it, but I didn't—I knew he'd done stuff, but I didn't know he'd done something like that.

I knew he understood grief. I didn't know that it had spilled out of him and into the world.

I didn't know he had hurt people other than himself.

He nods. "And I—well, you know I kept stealing cars after that. My parents kept as much of it as quiet as they could—they paid off the guy I hit and managed to cut deals for the other cars up until the bus thing."

My throat feels tight, gummy. "Why?"

"Because my dad wants to be a judge and he had a pretty good chance of becoming one until the bus. I did that on a Tuesday, during school, and it caused a lot of problems."

"I remember," I say, thinking back. We'd all had to wait an extra hour to leave school, even the people with cars, because the bus had to be brought back, and even then the school board was afraid to use it until a group of mechanics looked it over. They ended up readjusting all the school bus routes so the kids on the bus Caleb stole could be put onto others and still get home. "You got sent away after that, right?"

"Yeah. I've never told anyone about the guy. Not even the therapists at suck camp. I...anyway, my parents have plenty of reasons to hate me that aren't about Minnie." He pushes his hair off his face and blinks hard, looks toward the door. "You probably want to go back to school now."

Part of me wants to. Caleb Harrison understands me, but he isn't—he truly can't help me. I thought I got that before, but I didn't.

I do now.

Caleb understands me because he's still hurting too. I thought he was a victim, that he lashed out because his parents blamed him for his sister's death. And they did, and he did—he took all their hate and tore himself apart over it—but he isn't innocent. He did things, awful things.

But I look at him, standing in this tiny white room, and he is the loneliest person I have ever seen. He has nothing. No one.

And I know how that feels.

I get up and walk over to him. And then, like he did last night, I put my arms around him.

He stiffens for a second and then he hugs me back, his arms wrapping tight around me. I feel him shaking and rest my head on his shoulder.

"Emma," he says, just a whisper, and that's all he says. But I hear it, and I don't let go.

28

We drive back to school the same way we left, in silence, but his voice catches me as I'm getting out of the car.

"Emma, I just want you to know that what I did, I wish it hadn't happened. That's the worst part. Because the liv—"

"The living with it is forever," I say, and when he looks at me, I see that he will always have ghosts.

But I also see that he has carried them by himself and that he knows what he's done, who he is, and he is trying to live with it. With himself, and with the world he has.

I see that he is beautiful. Not just outside, but inside, under the mistakes and anger and grief, is a heart that beats pure and true. That loves his sister and his parents and wishes for things that can't ever be.

He wants things to be whole, but knows they can't. He sees that, and doesn't look away.

"I'm going to fail all my classes this term," I tell him. "I won't do the things I thought I would, won't go to the college I used to want to. It all seems so stupid now that my mother's gone." I swallow. "The night before she died, I blew her off to do homework. I thought I'd always...I thought there would be other times. But there aren't, and that's the worst. That's the part I hate most."

I look at him, and I don't wonder if he'll understand. I know grades and the plans I'd made, the way I tried to build a future that would be glowing, perfect, is something he's never thought about. He never had the time. The chance.

But I know he understands about seeing all the things you lost, the moments you thought you'd have, the ones you were so sure of. I know he gets that there is a moment you never saw, a moment that just came, and that it's unmade and remade you. That you can't be who you used to be once it's happened.

He leans toward me and touches my hair, my nonbeautiful, noncurly hair, and looks at me. At my face, which has no tri-fecta, which is just a face and nothing more until he touches it, one finger sliding down my cheek to my jaw.

And then, for a moment, I do feel different. Not beautiful, not something as simple as that.

I feel special. I feel like there is the world, and then there is Caleb and me. Just us, a broken little party of two but it isn't so bad, being broken. Not with someone who under-stands. Not with him.

"I didn't expect you," he says, and then he presses his forehead against mine, his eyes closed. "I don't know what to do."

I look at him and I understand, but part of me wants there to be more. Wants to be special beyond the understanding we share.

Part of me just wants him to want me.

"I should go," I say because I have felt want and it didn't do me any favors and Mom is dead and Caleb isn't going to save me and I don't know if I should trust myself because I used to believe that to have the perfect life, I just needed to study and work hard.

And look where that got me.

I get out of the car and head into school. I don't look back, but I spend what's left of the day hiding in one of the girls' bathrooms and thinking about him.

It's actually a relief when the final bell rings and I go out and find Dan. I don't understand this part of me, the thing inside me that has let me think about something other than Mom. I know that I am still living but it hasn't—

It hasn't been like this.

At the hospital, I sit in the cafeteria, a fruit cup smelling of canned pineapple in front of me.

I see Caleb's cart after Dan comes to get me, as I'm walking to Mom.

I stop. I pull the package of cotton candy out of my bag, the one from this morning, put it on the cart and then I go see her.

When I sit down, I tell her everything.

"Are you mad?" I say, and I don't think she would be, but

she would be worried. She wanted me to be safe, to be with a guy like Dan or my father.

My father, who died, and Dan.

Dan, who did this.

"Would you—?" My voice breaks, and I hold her hand tight. Will her to somehow hear me. To show me a sign. Something, anything.

She's silent, but her belly ripples. I swallow and close my eyes.

29

I see Caleb the next day, as I'm standing by Olivia's locker before first period.

"So you were really quiet last night," she's saying and I nod because I was. Olivia came over and talked about Roger and asked about Mom, and then she painted her fingernails with magic markers I bought to do a project I know I signed up for but remember nothing about.

She's still talking, and I see Caleb and I know he sees me and I like that I know that, that I see him seeing me, and then he is coming over.

I am watching him walk toward me and we have talked, I have told him things I haven't even told Olivia, but we haven't really talked at school.

We haven't talked where everyone can see us.

"Hey," he says and his hair is in his face again. I tilt my own head back so I can see him a little better and catch his grin, slight and embarrassed, and he pushes his hair back, those cheekbones a little red. "Thanks for...you know."

I think he means yesterday but he could also mean the cotton candy or both, but I feel people looking at us and I know I have to say something. "Sure."

His grin grows wider but his eyes get serious, and now I know what he means. He means yesterday. His house, his life. The truths he told.

How I stayed after I heard them.

He moves a little, his hair starting to fall forward, and I reach out and touch one side of it, the curls sliding over my fingers.

We both still and I feel the same jolt I did yesterday, only now it's stronger.

It's stronger and it's confusing but I don't want to turn away.

He stares at me and I am staring back and he leans in a little, leans in toward me, and I could touch his face, I could slide my hand so it would rest on the line of his jaw, like he touched me before. I could—

"Emma?" Olivia says, and she sounds beyond surprised.

Caleb shakes his head, like he's surfacing from underwater, and his hair falls over his face as my hand slides away.

"See you later?" he says.

I nod.

"What was *that*?" Olivia says after he goes.

"Talking."

"Uh-huh. You touched his hair! What's going on? Are you and Caleb hanging out now?"

I think of him asking me if I wanted to go yesterday. Of how he shook when I held him. Of how he'd whispered my name.

"Yeah, we are."

"You sure you want to?" Olivia says, and when I don't say anything, she sighs. "I know everything with your mom is terrible, but Caleb? He steals cars!"

"There's more to him that that. He gets everything that's going on."

"And I don't."

"You do, but not like he does. He gets how it feels. Everything with the baby, it's—"

"*He.* You know that the baby is a boy, but you don't say that. Why?"

I don't say, because then it's not just about what Dan did. How he never even asked me, just made his choice. "He, he, *he.* There. Better?"

"No because it's like you don't think about anything but what Dan did and well—it's weird how you don't talk about how you're going to have a brother, you know? And now Caleb Harrison?"

"You don't even know how well I know all about it. About him. It's *all* about him, and you don't have to sit in the hospital and look at your dead mother every day."

"Okay, okay, sorry," Olivia says, her mouth trembling. "I just…I don't know. I want to make things better for you."

I put my arm through hers. "I know you do."

But the thing is, she can't. Not like she wants to.

No one can make things better, but Caleb…Caleb gets it in a way no one else does.

30

The afternoon drive to the hospital is the same as always, but the visit isn't. There is a doctor waiting for us when we get to the floor where Mom is, and I see Dan stiffen.

There is only one reason a doctor waits to see you.

"Mom?" I say, my voice breaking. "What's wrong with Mom?"

I know she's gone, I do, but I've gotten used to seeing her, to touching her even if she can't feel it, and I suddenly don't want what I've been so sure I do. I don't want to hear that she's gone forever and ever, that the machines stopped holding on to her, that she slipped away and all that's left is the ground and the goodbyes all over again but without her there, without me seeing her every day.

"No," Dan says, "oh no, no, no," and I realize the doctor

is talking, that he's saying, "Lisa's holding steady," and then I know it's the baby.

Mom's belly, her swollen, fluttering belly, and what's inside, what Dan wants, what he's done, and the doctor is still talking but I'm not listening because Mom is still here, I can still see her. She's here, right here.

I start to walk toward her. I want to see her now, I have to see her now, but a nurse touches my arm and steers me behind Dan, and the doctor is still talking, saying, "fetal distress" and "fluid levels" and Dan is crying.

"What's going to happen?" he says, and all the talk afterward drifts over me because I forgot what I realized the day I was in Caleb's room, when I learned he wasn't going to save me, that he couldn't make all my pain go away.

Under the idea that we can all make our fates, that we have choices, is the reminder that sometimes we don't. That sometimes life is bigger than our plans. Bigger than us.

I look at Dan, who is still crying, and I reach over and touch his hand. He grabs my fingers and holds on, tight.

I don't try to pull away.

We wait, first with the doctor and then in the waiting room.

"Thank you, Emma," Dan says. "Thank you for being here."

"I—" I start to say, and then the doctor comes back in. He is smiling now and then Dan is standing up, crying again but hugging the doctor and saying "Thank you" over and over again.

"We're still not out of the woods," the doctor says. "But

you can go see her now. Just one visitor, though. We still are monitoring the baby very closely."

"The baby," Dan says, grinning, and then he turns to me and says, "I'm so glad you understand now. This is really what Lisa wanted, and now our son—"

"I want to see her," I say, and Dan, Dan who was just hugging me, who held my hand, who I once thought loved Mom more than anything, who I thought would put her and me first because he said he would says, "Emma, I have to see her."

I walk out of the waiting room then. I watch Dan come out. I watch him walk toward Mom's room. He looks at me before he does and I stare back at him until he turns away.

He doesn't ask me to come with him.

He is crying again, though, but I don't care, I don't care, I don't care.

It's not the first time he's done something without talking to me. It's not the first time he's acted like I don't matter to him.

When he comes back out I walk toward the elevator because I know he will come, he will drive us both back to the house, and he got his way again. He gets his baby, his precious son, and sometimes life is bigger than our plans but Dan's are safe.

Caleb is in the elevator, along with a woman in a wheelchair. He sees me and his eyes go wide. I see everything in them. Worry. Care.

Dan isn't even looking at me. He is staring at the floor, he is looking at the elevator ceiling, anywhere but at me, and

I hate him. I hate that Mom ever met him and that I once loved him.

I feel fingers touching mine and I know it's Caleb, that he's behind me and that he's reached out, stretched his fingers so they'll touch mine.

I reach back and hold on.

And when the elevator dings and the doors open, I turn around and hug him. I lean into him and say, "Thank you," and then I pull away and walk past Dan, who is looking at me and I dare him to say something, anything, with my eyes.

He doesn't.

31

That night I sleep in Mom's room. I lie in the bed she slept in, I put my head on her pillow. I knock Dan's pillow onto the floor. He doesn't sleep in here anymore anyway; he hasn't since the day Mom died. He sleeps downstairs or sometimes, I think, in the nursery.

The phone rings, and neither of us answers it. I think I hear a noise on the roof at one point but I don't get up. I just want to get through tonight, and there is no room in my heart or head for anything or anyone else but Mom.

And my anger.

I find Caleb as soon as I get to school in the morning, though, wade past the people in the halls and slip into a space next to his locker. He smiles when he sees me.

I smile back, but I know it is shaking.

"Hey," he says. "What happened yesterday?"

"Problem with the baby."

"Oh. Is everything okay?"

"For now."

"Your stepdad seemed pretty wrecked."

"He should," I say, and hear the bitterness in my voice.

"I came by last night," he says. "But you didn't come out on the roof."

"No," I say, and Caleb touches my arm. I feel it under my clothes, under my skin, I feel his touch seep into my body, beat through me to the thrum of my blood pulsing.

"Angry or scared?"

"Both."

"I'll be there today," he says. "At the hospital, I mean." He clears his throat. "You know that already. I—uh, I really wanted to do more yesterday. I haven't felt like that in a long time."

And then he says, "Is it true that you and Anthony were together?"

I stare at him, shocked. "Anthony?" Why are we talking about Anthony?

"Yeah. The guy who knows everything and talks all the time. I just...I heard some stuff."

"Stuff?" I knew Anthony would have talked—that's what he does—he talks and talks and I bet he said, "I like Emma, but when she asked for a physical relationship, I felt that it was the wrong choice for both of us. She did understand that, eventually, although she was rather emotional about it."

I thought I was okay with that. I really did. I certainly pictured him saying it. I just never pictured Caleb hearing it, or me caring about Caleb hearing it.

But I do. I really do.

"He didn't want me," I mutter. "Okay? That's the whole story."

"Anthony's an idiot," he says.

"Oh." I know I am blushing, I can feel how hot my face is. I wish I hadn't told him Anthony didn't want me. Not that it matters, except it does.

"Emma?" It's Olivia and I look around, see her staring at me and Caleb. At Caleb's hand, which is still on my arm, and my hand, which is somehow now resting on it.

"Hey," I say, and Olivia looks at Caleb, eyebrows raised, and Caleb sighs, not with anger, but with resignation, and whispers, "I'll come find you later, okay?"

"Hi, Olivia," he says as she comes up to us.

"Hi," she says, and she's not being mean but she definitely doesn't look or sound friendly and Caleb vanishes into the crowd of people moving through the hall.

"Okay, you and Caleb are more than just friends."

"We're not." Not really.

"Then what's with all the staring and the touching?"

"He had his hand on my arm."

"I haven't seen him touch anyone in....well, forever," Olivia says. "Look, are you sure he knows you're just friends? I mean, he's Caleb, you know? Druggie. Car thief."

"He's still a person."

"I know, but what if he's trying to—?"

"You aren't going to say 'take advantage,' are you?"

"All right, that might be melodramatic, but—"

I cut her off. "Look, it's Caleb, the guy who is the trifecta, right? So Caleb and me? Anthony didn't even want me, Olivia. Come *on*."

"He doesn't look at you like Anthony did."

Anthony's an idiot.

I clear my throat, and know I'm blushing again because she's right.

Anthony never, ever once looked at me like Caleb does.

Olivia looks at me. "I don't want you to get hurt."

"It's not like that," I say, and it isn't. Not like how Olivia means. Because of yesterday, and how I learned you can break all over again even when you think you can't. Because I'm not the girl I was, the one who looked at Anthony and saw what I wanted to see and nothing more. I had that luxury, that belief that the future could be whatever I wanted.

I know better now. I saw who Anthony was—too late, but I saw it—and I see who Caleb is. He made me see all of him, everything, and I want to keep looking.

32

Dan tries to say something to me on the way to the hospital after school.

"I was worried yesterday," he says. "Upset. And if I scared you or made you angry, that's okay." He stares straight ahead at the traffic. "I know you wanted to see your mother. Please don't think I don't know how much you love her."

"But you needed to see her," I say. "Check on what's inside her."

"Your brother."

"You were there to see the baby as much as her. Maybe more," I say.

Dan shakes his head and says, "That's not true. How can you even think that?"

I laugh and it's so harsh and bitter it makes my own heart contract.

But it does shut Dan up.

"Thirty-three days," I say when we get to the hospital. "That's how I think it. Why I think it. Come find me when I'm allowed to see her. You'll let me do that today, won't you? Now that you've got the all-clear on what *you* want."

I start to move away but Dan grabs my arm.

"Emma, instead of running away, why don't we talk?"

The doctor comes out, catches Dan's eye, and I hear him suck in a breath. I pull away.

I walk away.

Dan doesn't come after me.

I don't sit in the waiting room. I can't. Not today, not with Dan and the empty words he wants me to hear.

I'm seventeen. I'm supposed to have my future mapped out—what college I'll go to, what major I'll have, what job I want. I'm supposed to even see past that, to the job I'll get, to the life I'll have on my own.

All that, and I can't see my own mother. Because I'm just a kid, and Dan is her husband. I'm not an adult, I don't have an equal say. I've never had one in what's happened. Not once, and why? Dan was her husband but I'm—I was—her daughter. It's not fair that all I've gotten to be is just *here*. I don't want that.

I want someone to hear me.

I want Dan to care what I think.

No, I wanted him to care.

I can't take this.

I head out of the hospital and walk into the parking lot. A parking lot should look the same everywhere but this one is somehow more depressing, as if all the cars are tainted by what's inside. Sickness, or the potential of it. The worry. The waiting. The fear. Even the light reflecting off the windshields isn't warm or comforting. It just hits my eyes and makes them sting.

I rub them, and then pinch the bridge of my nose. I will see Mom today. I will. Somehow I will make it happen—and then I see Caleb in the parking lot, standing by a blue car.

His car isn't blue.

He doesn't see me, and I look at him. He is staring at the car like it's more than a car, like he sees something in it or around it. That he somehow needs it.

He rubs a hand along one window, fingers tracing down to the door handle. He pulls on it like it will open but it doesn't.

"Hey," I say, and he doesn't turn away from the car. He is still touching the handle and his other hand is shaking. I can see that even from here.

"Caleb?" I say, and walk over to him.

He doesn't seem to hear me.

"Caleb?" I say again, and he turns, his eyes wild, wide and unfocused, like he's not really here. One hand tests the handle again and his other hand is still shaking. I watch his gaze skim over the ground, all flat and paved over except for a few places where the concrete edging has chipped away, fallen free.

I swallow. "Why this car?"

"What?" His voice is distant, like he isn't here.

"Why do you want to steal this car?"

He looks at me then, and I look back at him steadily even

though I'm shaking inside now, startled by this glimpse of a Caleb I knew about, but that I've never seen.

He still looks alone, but now there is anger in his eyes too.

"I…my mother," he says slowly, like the words are painful to say, like it hurts him to say them. "She was here just now, visiting a client. I saw her in the hall. She said, 'Try not to screw this up,' and she didn't even look at me. She never looks at me." He laughs, and the sound is so fake and bitter that I get goose bumps.

"I'm sorry."

"Are you going to try to stop me?"

"No. Someone I—someone I like told me they couldn't tell me how to be okay. I'm pretty much in the same place."

He blinks, then looks back at the car. "I'd probably get sent away again. I'd be out of the house. They wouldn't have to see me. I wouldn't have to see them."

He blows out a breath, and then looks at me again. "I really want to do it, Emma."

"But suck camp sucked, remember?"

"Yeah," he says. "But I also wouldn't be able to talk to you anymore, and I'd miss that. I'd miss you."

Anthony said I was lovely once, and I felt such warmth, such gratitude. I thought it was want.

It wasn't. Want is what hits me now, and it is not lovely or even pleasant. It's hard and fast and it hurts. My insides cramp with it, and a thousand images I didn't know I could even think of race through my mind.

"I'd miss you too," I say, because it is all I can say, because in my mind Caleb is not standing near me, he is next to me, twined around me, and there is no car, there is no pain, there is just us, and I—

I want a broken former car thief who still wants to steal cars but who just said he won't because if he did, he'd miss me.

"You didn't want to hear that," he says, and I shake my head because it's not that, it's *so* not that.

But yet it is because I've seen what wanting does.

My mother wanted Dan and when she died, he ignored how scared she was, how she used to rub her belly with her eyes closed like she was wishing for it all to work out for what he wants. For his son.

I take a deep breath, and then I tell Caleb the truth. "You confuse me."

I look at him and my heart, which I was so sure was dead, burned out, beats hard and fast. Beats like I'm alive, like there is life in me, like I didn't die when Mom did.

"So I guess I'm not taking this car," Caleb says, and lets go of the handle. "And just so you know, you confuse me too."

"I know," I say, and when he smiles at me I want things to be simple, I want him to be a guy, a regular guy, and I want to be a girl who knows she will go home to her mother and a stepfather she knows and loves but—

But that's not how things are.

It's not how life is.

I feel his smile then. I don't just see it anymore. It crawls inside me, curls up alongside all my grief. Confuses me, just like I said.

"We go inside now, right?" Caleb says, and we do. Silent, together but not, walking side by side but not touching.

He takes the elevator up to the floor where Mom lies, and I look at him when I get off. He starts to wave, and then pushes his way off, stands next to me.

"Your mom," he says. "How is she?"

"I haven't seen her yet."

"Will you?"

"I don't know."

"Do you want—can I wait with you?"

I look at him and we smile at each other.

And so we sit in the waiting room, his foot pushing the cart I saw so much significance in that first day, back and forth.

"Do you need to go to other floors?"

"Yeah," he says, but he doesn't leave and I'm glad. It's nice not to be alone.

Dan comes in, looks at Caleb, and then says, "You can see her, Emma, but just for a minute. She's tired."

Caleb gets up when I do and Dan looks at both of us. Says, "Emma, I haven't really met your friend."

"This is Caleb," I say, as Caleb nods at Dan and walks out. "And Mom isn't tired. She's dead. You know it. I know it."

I head toward Mom, and Dan follows me. I hear him breathing.

"Her body is tired, Emma," he says, and he sounds weary, on the edge of tears. "The baby is still in trouble and things aren't as good as they could be. The risk of infection is even worse now and the doctors..."

He keeps talking but I ignore him and sit next to Mom. She is even thinner now. I look at her belly. It's still swollen. Round.

"Hey, Mom," I say, and take her hand. It lies heavy and cool in mine. "I missed you yesterday. I know you're gone, but when I see you I can…" I trail off, look over at Dan.

He doesn't leave.

"Dan's here," I say. "He's watching over what you worked so hard for. I still remember what you told me that time you had to go on bed rest. How you hated the thought of having to lie still. Of how trapped you felt. You wanted to go downstairs but Dan wouldn't let you. He was okay with you moving around after you got the clot taken out but once you were pregnant with his baby he…"

Dan leaves then and I blow out a breath.

"Mommy," I whisper. "I need you. I don't understand anything anymore. Yesterday, when the doctor said something to Dan I thought you were gone. I forgot that you are." I press my forehead to hers and pretend there are no tubes, no machines, that the skin under mine can feel my touch.

It's easy to. I want some part of her to be here. I hadn't realized how much.

And even though she's gone, I don't want to let her go.

I don't know if I can.

33

"You know that I respect your privacy," Dan says on the way home. "I let you lock yourself in your room all the time. But today, with your mother—look, everything is very fragile right now."

"You mean with the baby," I say, and it costs me to get that last word out.

"Why do you do that?" Dan says. "Your brother is fighting for his life, and you talk about him like he's not real. I don't like that."

When I don't say anything, he looks over at me, a quick, incredulous glance. "You were excited about the baby, I know you were. Don't you see that he's family? That he might have your mother's eyes or her smile, that he'll be a way for us to always remember her?"

"I know," I say, and I want to sound calm but I don't, I hear how high my voice is, I hear how angry it is. "I know she'll live through him. I heard you back when you made your choice."

"It's not just my choice."

It was, and it is, and we both know it.

"Emma, it really wasn't and isn't just my choi—"

"Shut up," I say, and I'm screaming now, I feel the vibration of the words roaring up my throat and out of me. "Shut up, shut up, shut up! I am so tired of you talking. I'm so tired of you."

"Tough, because I'm not going anywhere and you don't get to talk to me like that."

Dan pulls into the driveway.

"Yeah, I do," I say as I open my door and get out, not caring that the car isn't even stopped, that I fall as I do, that I tumble onto the ground. I just want to be away from him. He stops the car, gets out and calls after me but I'm already in the house, running up the stairs and into my room, bolting the door closed behind me.

Let him call the police and have them come break down the door. Let him try it. I'm ready. I sit on my bed, fists clenched, waiting.

Dan knocks on the door.

"Emma, I know you're angry, but it can't be an excuse anymore." I hear the Dan I used to think I knew, the one who sat with me after Olivia and I went to the eighth grade dance and Olivia got asked to dance three times and I didn't get asked once. Dan didn't say things would be better in the morning or lies like that. He just hugged me and then served ice cream for breakfast, telling Mom, "It's got calcium, and sometimes people deserve something fun because they're special."

I'd told Mom about the dance too, and she'd rubbed my back and told me she loved me and it had been nice. But Dan really made me feel like everything was okay. Like I was okay. Like I was special.

I miss him. I hate that.

I grit my teeth and go out onto the roof just in time to see someone—Caleb?—walking toward the edge of it.

"Hey," I say.

"Hey."

"Olivia?"

"Hi," she says, turning around and coming back. "I was up here when you came in. Should I go?"

"Why?"

"You got out of a moving car, Emma. You looked pissed as hell and you ran into the house and I figured you and Dan would be talking."

"We're not."

"Oh," she says. "So, do you want me to stay?"

"Yeah. You know you don't even have to ask that."

Olivia sits down. "You sounded like maybe you wanted someone else to be out here."

I clear my throat. "Did I?"

She looks at me. I rub one foot along the shingles, hear the scrape against the bottom of my shoe. "All right. I saw Caleb at the hospital and I thought for a second that he was here. But I am glad to see you."

"Yeah?"

"Yeah," I say, and she bumps her foot with mine. "What happened today at the hospital?"

"Mom's...well. You know. But there are some problems with the baby and Dan wasn't even going to let me see her by myself."

"Why?"

"Stress. As if she can be stressed. It's like he forgets she's gone, and yesterday I realized I have too. I mean, I know she is, but I can see her, and..." I wipe my eyes. "I'm so tired of crying. Tell me something. Talk about you. Please."

"But—"

"Olivia, I need normal. You don't know how much I need it."

"Well my parents are both working, of course, and both coming home late—server problems again. Or something. I try not to absorb the tech talk. Oh, and Roger and I made out after school." She says the last bit with so much glee she's practically vibrating with it.

"Where?"

She blushes. "My car."

"Your car? What happened?"

"Well, we were talking after the last bell rang and he said he was going to get a ride home with his friend Ivan and I said, 'Oh, I can give you a ride home,' and he smiled at me like I was the last day of school and once we got in the car, stuff just happened."

"In the parking lot?"

"A little bit," she says, blushing. "And then I drove him to his house and we might have made out some more. Until his little brother came home and found us."

"He didn't!"

"Yeah, he did. But Roger was so great about it. He was nice to his brother but also got him to, you know, go, and then he said he'd call me and that he wanted to see my phone. I've told him about it."

"So, he wants to see your room."

"He said *phone*," Olivia says, but she's grinning. "It was just the most amazing afternoon." She looks at me. "You can't really want to hear this. I sound so shallow."

"You sound happy. Normal, remember?"

"But—"

"Nope. You sound happy and I'm glad you are and that you told me about it. And I want more updates, especially if room viewing is involved."

"You sure?"

"I need this. I don't want to forget that people have actual lives." It's what I don't have, and hearing about Olivia washes over me like rain, covering the thing I limp through every day, the thing that passes for a life but isn't one.

"Well, then I promise you'll hear if there's any room viewing. Which there won't be because I want more than just a thing, you know? I'd like an actual boyfriend. Not that I'm ruling out room viewing, but it's way down the line and… okay, now I'm totally wondering what he'd think of my room. And what it would be like to have him in it."

She leans back, shaking her head. "How am I supposed to be picking out which colleges I'm going to apply to when I just want to see if Roger is willing to go out with me this weekend. And next weekend. And also make out with me. Argh! I need to do something to get my mind off him."

"No haircuts. Or dying of hair."

"I wasn't going to do that. I could get bangs though, right? Bangs aren't a haircut."

"No bangs! You so need a different stress outlet, and no, I don't mean new eyeliner."

"I already bought some," she says and when I give her a look says, "What? I was a little wound up after I left Roger's house. Do you think he'll call tonight?"

"If he looked at you like you're the last day of school, then yeah, he'll call."

"I thought getting a guy to like you was the hard part," she mutters. "But it's just as hard after that. How come no one ever tells you that?"

"I think there's a lot of things that no one ever tells you," I say, and Olivia puts an arm around me, pulling me close.

We sit in silence until she says she has to go.

"Thank you," I say when she gets up, and she says, "Oh yeah, you thank me. I haven't shut up, and all I've talked about is Roger."

"Thank you," I say again and she hugs me, hard, before she starts to climb off the roof. I watch until she's gone.

Until I can't see anything.

34

Dan doesn't come back to my room and I go through the motions of getting ready for bed—the face washing, the teeth brushing—before I give up and crawl into bed, pissed-off. I know I won't sleep. I felt okay when Olivia was here, when I could hear about her life and not think about mine, but now I'm just hungry and still angry.

And lonely.

I always thought of grief as a blow that took everything out of you. And it is like that. But it stays, past that first hard hit. It stays and blows its breath into you.

It is always there, reminding you of what you've lost. What's gone.

I sit up for a while, reading a book Mom got me last year at Christmas, a huge story about a girl and a dragon and a prince that she ends up having to save. "You can't read school stuff all the time," she'd said, and I'd thanked her for the book and never opened it. I didn't want stories. I wanted grades, and good ones at that. I wanted a future.

Inside she'd written, *A story can take you anywhere. XO Forever, Mom.*

I didn't see it until I opened the book just a few minutes ago and I wish my story wasn't—

I wish it wasn't this one, and that's grief blowing softly over me again. Reminding me all over again.

I missed so many things with Mom.

I drop the book on my bed. I won't do this, I won't cry, I will just be glad I saw what she wrote now.

And I am. But I still wish I'd seen it before. That I'd known I needed to treasure every second I had, that I should focus on everything she said and did so I could always remember.

My stomach rumbles and I look at my door. Past it is the house. Past it is Dan.

When my stomach rumbles again, I get up. It's after midnight now. Dan will be asleep, on the sofa or in his office or in the nursery. I don't know why he doesn't sleep in Mom's bedroom anymore. I'm just glad there's something of Mom he's left alone. That he hasn't used for what he wants.

I open my door and go out into the hall. I go because I'm hungry and because I want to prove I can. I'm not afraid of anything Dan might say, because I've heard it all before and it's just words. Syllables and letters adding up to his choice and nothing more.

And I don't miss him that much. Not really.

Then I hear the humming.

I freeze, sure I'm hearing things; a ghost, a dream, that I'm asleep and back in a different time, back in a different me.

But I'm not hearing things. I'm in the hallway, in the dark, and my mother is dead and Dan is in the nursery, humming.

Dan used to hum a lot. All the time, in fact. I noticed it when he and Mom first started going out, the weird thing he did, how he hummed sometimes, and then I realized when he did it.

He hummed when he was doing something that made him happy.

He hummed when he was happy, and so he was always humming around Mom. And even me. Mom made him happy. We made him happy, and I used to love to hear him hum, loved waking up and going downstairs to Mom blinking sleep from her eyes as she rushed off to work, Dan humming as he urged her to eat something and talked about what he'd be working on that day, in his office in the house. "I like working at home," he'd say. "It's quiet, I get a lot done, and whenever I want, I can just step out into the hall and see signs of my family."

He made Mom's habit of dropping things—shoes, suit jackets, towels—sound like it was beautiful. He picked up after her. He picked up after me. He never told me to clean my room like Mom did. He just…he hummed, and was happy, and I knew it meant he loved us.

I lean against the wall now, my head spinning, my insides twisting, and yes, he really is humming.

I creep down the hall, one step, two steps, silent as can be.

He's in the nursery.

There is one light on, the light Dan put in by the changing table. It casts shadows everywhere, up and down the walls, dark lines and shapes, but it shows Dan clearly.

It shows Dan, and he is putting a crib together.

He's putting it together and he looks happy and he's humming.

He is happy. I know what his humming means because I know him. I spent years loving him, trusting him, and now he is humming and then he whispers something.

Whispers, "Lisa."

He whispers Mom's name and he isn't humming anymore. His voice is soft, sad, sorry, and no, no, no, no. *NO.*

He said her name like he loves her, like he's sorry, and I am gone now, I am slipping away, quietly heading downstairs and out of the house, into the garage, my chest so tight I can't breathe.

I am seeing spots, I am dying, this is what happened to Mom and now it's happening to me. You walk downstairs and you're fine, everything's fine except maybe you know something is wrong, maybe you've said something to your daughter but you've been smiling and trying and you reach for the toast and then you die.

Just like that.

Except I don't.

I stand in the garage, and the tightness in my chest passes.

The memory of Dan humming doesn't, and neither does the sadness with which he said Mom's name.

I pace around the garage and find myself in front of the

fridge where Mom kept all the things she wasn't allowed to have after she got pregnant. Dan, who could never resist a sale at the grocery store, used to have it stocked with things he'd gotten "for practically free!" Mom and I made him stop that after eating pea soup two weeks in a row, but the fridge stayed.

It was from Dan's old apartment and Mom would stash tiny chocolate bars in it, and Dan would store leftovers, let them sit in the freezer till he'd eat them for lunch.

Mom cleaned the kitchen out after the first official week of pregnancy, sighing as she put things into bags and had me take them out here.

I never looked inside the bags. I didn't think about what pregnant women shouldn't eat. I didn't care. I just saw Mom, and she was there like she always was, doing what she always did, which was organizing things the way she wanted and I—

I never thought about what she gave up. Not until after she gave up her life.

I stare at the fridge, almost shaking, which is weird because it's food, just food, how could she have thought that would hurt her?

And then I open it.

I want to know what she was afraid of besides the baby.

And it's…it's cheese. A wheel of Brie, frozen and inedible. Some lunch meat. A piece of lamb all wrapped up and marked SMELLS HORRIBLE.

I don't feel better seeing this. She put away cheese and lunch meat and lamb? I see coffee too, but I remember that, suffered through two weeks of Mom switching to decaf and growling in the mornings.

I used to hide out in my room, wait until she was gone or just about to leave. I missed her on purpose.

I stand there, staring at this food, and it is just food, there are no secrets here, there is nothing of Mom here, and Dan was putting the crib together, I saw him, I saw it.

And then I see the bottle of wine.

35

Mom wasn't much of a drinker. She liked sweet drinks, the ones that come in frosted glasses and are tinted blue or green. Once Dan was around, he found her true weakness, which was for wine that smelled like fruit punch. I still remember the faces he'd make when he'd bring a bottle home, how he'd mock grimace when he'd open it and pour her a glass, shaking his head when she'd offer him one.

"Too sweet," he'd say. "Wine shouldn't taste like sugar."

Mom would shake her head and say, "Why would I want to drink something that is supposed to taste like oak or peat? I like what I like."

"I know you do," Dan would say and Mom smelled sweet, like fruit, when she kissed me after drinking her wine, and her smile would be softer somehow, as if all the things she worried about had been lifted away.

She drank a wine that came in a bottle with a picture of strawberries on it, and I pick it up now and stare at the top, think of how Dan used to say wine should have corks and Mom would say, "Okay for you, not okay for me." And they'd look at each other and there was so much love there.

At least, I thought there was.

The bottle isn't full. Mom must have had a glass, back before my bro—the baby—swam inside her. She came home from work and Dan opened the bottle and she drank a glass and maybe kissed me and smelled sweet and I don't remember it at all.

I was probably doing homework and was annoyed by the distraction. Annoyed by my mother wanting to see me. To pay attention to me.

I was so stupid.

I pick up the bottle. I open it, unscrewing the top, and take a sip. It is sweet, just like fruit punch, just like Dan always said, and Mom drank from this bottle. I have another sip and another and another until I am loose-limbed, breathing easy and the air smells like fake strawberries and Dan's humming seems far away. It doesn't hurt so bad.

I look at the bottle. It's almost empty, and I lift it up and swallow the last sip. The world is light now, I am light, and things are bad—they are—but I don't feel so bad. I feel like I could float up out of the house and into the sky. Up into Mom.

I wish Caleb was here. He'd know how it feels to want to

float up. And he's so pretty, those cheekbones, those eyes, the hair he hides behind that I touched but not like I wanted to.

I can admit it now, it's easy. I want to have his hair in my hands while he holds me.

I should go see him. It's not that far. I can walk there. I can leave through the garage side door and Dan doesn't keep me prisoner here. I spend more time worrying that he'll decide he doesn't want me than I want to think about and...

No.

I don't want to think.

I look at the strawberries on the wine bottle again. They are happy-looking. I didn't know strawberries could look happy.

I want to be happy. That would be so nice, to be happy.

I'd feel happier if I left the house, so I go outside, and there I am, just me and the night. Well, and the bottle, but it is so light in my hands and I am so light, I'm almost flying, sort of. I don't even have to walk down the street, my feet are just going, going, going and they know where to go.

Caleb's house is even bigger in the night, all huge and dark and I was there, I went in there, and I held his hand and he is so alone and I am so alone. I look at the garage with my feet on the ground but not really on it because I feel so free, I am just me, I am not—

I am not sad.

And I see things too. I see a door on the side of the garage, just like on mine, and I open it. It's dark inside and there are cars and I bet one of them replaced the one Caleb drove into the lake because his parents don't know it's not about the cars. They don't see, but then adults never see anything, it's like you get old and you don't see how things are, you just see how you want them to be. Dan does that, he did that, and I don't want to think about Dan.

So I won't. I'll just be here, in this garage, and I am walking up Caleb's stairs which are so tall and deep I don't quite know how to place my feet.

I think I'm drunk, but the thought passes through and floats away like all the others. Like how I'm sad and I miss Mom and Dan. Just thoughts, and it's hard to get up the stairs and I wish there was more wine. I wish I could taste strawberries and feel like I do now forever, plus I am going to see Caleb sleeping. He will have his eyes closed and he'll be surprised except I'll be quiet, so quiet he'll never know I am here and—

"Emma?" Light, bright light, making me blink.

It's Caleb. And he's awake.

36

"You're supposed to be asleep," I say, and Caleb stares at me.

"Are you—Emma, are you drunk?" he says and I shake my head because I don't drink, and how could a few sips of wine that tasted like fruit really make me drunk? To get drunk you have to drink beer or smelly liquor and lots of it. Standing in a garage with a bottle of wine can't get you drunk. Not that drunk, anyway.

"Yeah," Caleb says, "It can," and I say, "Wait, did I just say all that?" and he nods. He isn't wearing a shirt and he has nice chest muscles and he's nice and I like him.

"Okay, Emma, okay, stop and drink this," Caleb says and I take the glass of water that is suddenly right in front of me. I'm thirsty, but not super thirsty, but somehow the water is all gone and then there is another glass and I drink that too.

"You put a shirt on," I say to Caleb, who runs a hand

through his hair and looks at me like he hasn't ever done before, like I've made him happy and angry at the same time.

"You shouldn't have come here," he says and that is such a stupid thing to say that I tell him that and add, "Where else would I go? Who else understands? And besides, I wanted to see you," and he blinks and his eyes are closed and he has a shirt on but under it is skin—I know that—and I can feel it—yes, there it is, warm under my hand and he jerks back like I've hit him and says, "Emma, please."

"What?" I say, and I don't get it, doesn't he know how this feels? Doesn't he want to feel this way too?

Someone groans. It's not me. Is he sick? I look at him, but he looks okay. He looks great.

"I feel great," I say, and he shakes his head like he knows something I don't. I move toward him and he backs up but not fast, he backs up slow and I see his eyes and I'm not stupid.

"I never said you were stupid," he says and I guess I'm still talking but that's okay. I don't talk much, I keep so much inside, I am so full of things that hurt but they don't hurt now. I rest my head on his shoulder, brush my lips over his neck.

He tastes like salt, like tears. He tastes like pizza and grief and love and fear. He tastes like Caleb and I want more and there is a noise and it isn't me I am not saying anything now, I know I'm not, and I pull away and it's Caleb, he is making that noise, a broken, almost animal sound, his head thrown back and I can see a pulse beating in his neck. It's his heart and it is beating and I can make it beat fast and I like that and I move in again.

"Emma," he says, and he sounds so strange, so serious, and I poke his chest because he must get this, I know the things he used to do, he must have felt like this.

"Emma, you'll be sorry when you're sober," he says, and I look at him and say this—I know I say this—I say, "Why would I ever be sorry for you?" and his mouth brushes across my forehead, my cheek, my neck and I am turning toward him.

He is so close, he just needs to be a little closer, and my head hurts a little but not so bad. I still feel good and he feels good and I like that. I want it to keep going forever and ever.

"I can't," he says. "I don't—Emma, I don't want you to be sorry over me," and then we are lying down and he is closing his eyes and making soft, desperate noises as I press my face into his neck, his shoulder, and he is turning his mouth away from mine. When I say, "Why?" he says, "Just sleep, okay? Just sleep."

"I wanted the baby," I tell him, and I never meant to say that. I like to pretend I never thought that but I did, and I have said it now and I don't like this, I don't like it at all, and he says, "Hey, hey," his voice soft and I close my eyes and say, "Do you think that's why she died? Because I wanted the baby too?"

"No," he whispers. "No, it wasn't because of you. Don't ever think that."

"You won't kiss me," I whisper because I can and my eyes are heavy and the room is spinning and I don't feel bad but it's not like before. I am not floating. I remember things. I remember Dan and the crib and why I had to go.

"You don't want to kiss me," I say, and right before darkness falls he says, "I do. I really, really do," and I want to think about that but I can't, I can't focus like I want to.

But he said it.

37

I wake up during the night, twice, and throw up into Caleb's trash can.

He holds my hair back and I try not to feel like an idiot.

I do anyway.

"You aren't an idiot," he says, his hand rubbing warm circles on my back and I should be embarrassed that I'm still talking.

I'm not, though. I just feel...

Well, awful.

But nice too.

38

I have gotten straight A's every grading period since they started giving A's until…well, until. I wish there could be a line for that day, that moment where Mom left, something solid people could see.

So they could see that there is before Mom died, and that there is after.

The two don't connect. They can't. The person who could have held that time together is the reason why it's separate.

I always did the right thing. Before, before, before. That was my thing. Doing the right thing.

I have never had a drink, because it wasn't the right thing, and I wake up with my head pounding, a vicious, throbbing pain over my right eye, and my mouth tastes like someone stuffed it with smelly cotton balls and I am not at home.

I am lying on a narrow bed next to Caleb. He smells wonderful and looks wonderful and I know I don't. I also don't
have that moment you're supposed to have after you've been
drinking, the moment where you wonder what you did.

I know exactly what I did, what I said, and I am so humili-
ated I can feel my face, nuclear hot and practically glowing,
as I look at his closed eyes.

Which open and look right into mine.

"Hey," he says. "Need something for your head?" and it's
like everything is fine, like I didn't come over and throw myself at him but I did, I know I did, and maybe I didn't rip off
my clothes (thank goodness), but I wanted him and I know
he knows it and now—

"Emma," he says, and his hand is touching mine. He is
holding my hand and I want to die and I also want him to
keep holding my hand. "Stop worrying."

"I'm not. It's just that I should go."

I start to sit up but it hurts way too much to do that. Caleb
keeps holding my hand, and he is looking at me. He remembers last night—of course he does—he wasn't the one drunk
on a bottle of strawberry wine. He didn't act like an idiot.

And then he touches me. One hand on my neck, a mirror
of where my mouth touched his skin last night.

"Don't run," he says. "I've done that, and you just end
up back where you started. And I—" He breaks off, blushes
and I see the color on his face, his chest, and my body stirs.
It wasn't just last night and the wine that did it. It's him. He
does this to me, melts me all over.

"I don't want you to go yet," he says.

So I stay.

I stay, and we eat cold toaster pastries in the light of the rising sun and he gives me water and ibuprofen. We are silent but it's not a bad silent, it's a comfortable silent. I thought I'd have to run away, that being drunk and barging in to see him and all the other things meant I had to go.

When I tell him that he grins and he is so beautiful that I swallow and look at my hands.

"Since when have you done what you're supposed to?" he says.

"Since forever. At least until..." I trail off and all the hurt comes back, everything from last night comes back, Dan and the nursery. The crib.

I wish I hadn't seen it.

I wish I'd never wanted the baby but I did, and look what it cost.

Caleb hands me another cold toaster pastry.

"Here," he says, wrapping my fingers around it, but I can't eat anymore. I have to go home. I have to see Dan.

I have to talk to him.

This time, when I get up, Caleb doesn't stop me and I see the bed for the first time—really see it, I mean. It's tiny and we were there, we were both there, and I said—

"Last night—" I start to say, and he stands up too and says, "I know," and his voice is so serious and he is letting me know it's okay because this is what you do when you care about someone. You don't think me, me, me. You think you, you, you.

I could think that about him. I do think that, and I could think past that.

I could love him.

I think I already might, but I don't want to think about that now.

"I meant it," I say in a rush because it's Caleb and it's true. "I meant all of it." I know I am blushing, and I leave then because I can't say more, I don't want to say more, there is too much else going on and I shouldn't—

My mother is dead and I shouldn't feel.

But I do, and I look back when I leave. I watch him smile and see him wave at me.

And I smile and wave back.

39

I notice the sun again as I'm walking home. It surprises me like it did before, but this time I stop and look up at it. I know you're not supposed to do that, but all that radiant light. All that warmth. It's just there. Always there.

My vision is spotted when I look away, and it makes me a little dizzy. Well, that and the hangover, but it was worth it. All of it was worth it and today will be—

I haven't thought of a day that way, as what it will be, what it could be, since before Mom died. My days have just been what is.

I'm not happy, but I'm something close to it.

Then I walk into the house.

Dan is standing right by the door and says, "Emma?" like

he doesn't know me. His eyes are bloodshot, almost worried-looking, and when I say, "Yeah?" he just looks at me.

"Dan," I say slowly, heading toward the kitchen after a moment has passed and he's still staring. "Are you going to be okay to drive me to school?"

"But you…" Dan has followed me into the kitchen and he is speaking strangely, haltingly, like he is having a hard time finding words, and I know he knows that I left the house last night.

"I went for a walk," I say, because I have been walking and because the rest is mine. Dan has his nursery and his crib and his baby. I can have last night. The bad—and the good.

"You were gone all night. I've been sitting down here for hours waiting and worrying. Where were you?"

"Worrying?"

"Yes, worrying. Where were you?"

"I went to see a friend."

"Who? Not Olivia because when I called her she had no idea where you were." He leans in a little and then stills. "You've been drinking! That's—you can't do that!"

I shrug.

"I don't want this kind of thing to happen again. You need to talk to someone, and I think—"

"You've said that before. You say it a lot, actually. But you don't do anything, do you? It's all just pretend."

"Pretend? I've been up all night worried about you. Is that pretending?"

"You were up putting the crib together for your son," I say, and he stiffens.

"Where else is he supposed to sleep? And why is it always 'your son'? Why isn't it ever 'my brother'? Because he is, and your mother would have wanted—"

"What? This? She would have wanted to be dead? Oh yeah, Dan, she'd be so happy to see her body now. She'd be thrilled to know she's a collection of wires and machines for what *you* want."

"Your mother wanted—"

"Don't. You can say she did all you want but that doesn't make it true. She was dead, Dan. *Dead.* You didn't get to ask her what she wanted. You didn't know, and you don't know. You're just pretending. Again."

"No, *you* don't know what your mother wanted," he says, and stares at me so firmly, with such belief in his eyes, that I see where he's been able to find the strength to do this, to keep Mom's body lying there, dead but run by machines for the baby.

He truly believes this is what Mom would have wanted.

I shake my head at him. "No, see, you know what you wanted. You were there, you saw how scared she was about being pregnant. And you didn't and don't care."

"She was scared," he says, and I stare at him, shocked, my head starting to pound again and my stomach churning because he knew, he knew, he knew.

He knew she was scared.

"Lisa was terrified she'd never get pregnant," he says. "And then, when she did, she was terrified she'd lose the baby. She wanted him so much. Don't you remember how she'd sit with her hand over her stomach? Don't you know why she did that?"

My stomach churns again. I don't like what he's saying; he's twisting it all around, he's not saying she was scared like she actually was, he's making it sound like she—

Like she knew what he'd do if she died, and that she'd want it.

Like he knew her better than me.

"I saw her," I say, and I keep my words careful, because I did know her better. I was part of her. I was there every day all the years before Dan ever was.

I knew she loved him before she told him. She told me first, because she wanted to know how I felt.

Run, I should have said. *Run.*

But I didn't, and once upon a time Mom was with us and loved us and we loved her and I loved Dan and I believe he loved me and that should have been enough, that should have been everything, but it isn't and wasn't because life isn't like that.

"I saw her," I say again. "I saw how she spent two years trying to get pregnant. I heard her crying when she wasn't, when you were out getting groceries or working in the yard or getting your hair cut. She never cried in front of you, you know. She always smiled and said she knew it would happen and you'd smile. You don't know what it cost her to say that to you. You got to hear about all the risks. She lived with them, even when the clot made things even riskier."

He pales, but I'm not done. "And then she got pregnant. She wanted to make sure, but you started planning right away, you were celebrating when she was still waiting and she'd been waiting for years to be sure. Did you ever even think about what would have happened if she wasn't pregnant? Did you ever think about how she'd have felt, to see everything you wanted not come true?"

"I didn't know she cried," Dan says and his voice is cracking but I don't care. I am beyond pity now. He should have heard all of this long ago. He should have seen it but he closed his eyes and just saw what he wanted. He didn't see what Mom wanted.

"She knew what was coming," I say. "From the moment she got pregnant, she was worried, just like you say. But I saw everything, Dan. I saw how hard it was for her to smile. How she moved so slowly, like she was afraid to, and this was Mom, who could change a tire in under a minute and who refinished the floors all by herself who used to dance around the house. She never moved like she had to be afraid until she was pregnant, and you can pretend all you want, but she was scared. She sat with a hand on her belly because deep down, she knew. She *knew* she was going to die."

"She didn't ever think that," Dan says, standing up. "You can't really believe that. You—" He pauses, stares at me. "But you do. You think she believed our baby would kill her?"

"She never even talked about having it. She let you handle the nursery, and when you and I tried to get her to talk about names, she wouldn't. Don't you see what that was? Don't you get it?"

"She *was* scared," Dan roars, and then sinks to the floor, face in his hands. "Emma, she was scared, but not like you think.

She was scared she was going to lose the baby. She wanted to do all those things—the nursery, talk about names—but there had been so many lost babies by then. She used to lie next to me at night and say 'It was so easy with Emma. Maybe it was too easy. Maybe this is why it's so hard now.' She would say—"

He looks at me, tears in his eyes. "She would say, 'I'm not supposed to be this lucky.' She didn't think she deserved you and her life and we did talk about the baby. She wanted him, and she never believed she was going to die."

"Right. So, she didn't believe it, and she also said, 'Oh, by the way, if I die, please make sure to keep my body going, please hook me up to machines and tubes so I can have your baby, Dan.' Is that what she told you after she said she thought she was too lucky?"

"That's—"

"What? True? Not true? We both know she never got a say because she was scared and then she was dead. You chose for her and you want to pretend it's what she wanted but you don't know that. You can't ever know that."

"And you can't know she would have wanted your brother to die," he says. "Because that's what would have happened, and did you ever hear her wish him away? Did she ever tell you he was a mistake? Did she ever whisper that she didn't want him? We both know she was scared, but I know why and I did what I thought she'd want, and that was to save our son."

"You never even asked me," I say and the words come out in a rush, ripped from me, and he blinks.

"What?"

"You never asked me about Mom. You never—it was like you didn't even notice I was there, in the hospital, when they told us she was dead and then you left because the doctor called you over. You just chose, you chose the baby, and I see my dead mother every day, Dan. I'm seventeen and I see my dead mother and I miss her and I want her back but she can't come back. She'll just lie there till the doctor cuts her open and then her body won't be needed anymore, *you* won't need her anymore and it'll be you and your son. The perfect little family."

"Stop this," Dan says, moving over to the stove, his whole body shaking. "I have loved you since the moment you and your mother let me into your lives. I have always been proud to have you as my daughter but hearing you talk about your mother like this, like she's nothing to me, like it doesn't kill me to know that she's gone, like I don't miss her like you do or love her at all is bullshit. And you say 'me and my son,' but what about you? Is the idea of having a brother that bad? Are you that jealous?"

"Jealous? You think I'm *jealous?* Did you hear anything I just said? You *never* asked me what I wanted for Mom. You never ever asked me anything about her. I've hated the baby because Mom died and he lived, but he'll never…" I start to laugh then because he is so wrong, we are all so wrong and broken and I am not laughing so much as crying, I push away from the table and I am standing in the kitchen, I am looking at Dan and it is all pouring out, all of it, everything I've kept inside is pouring out.

"He'll never see her. Never, and when's the last time you

hugged me? Do you know, Dan? Because I do. It was the morning Mom died. After she died, you were there and I was there but it was like we didn't know each other. You made your choices and we came back here and that was it. You go through the motions, you take me to see Mom and talk about how worried you are. But I saw you in that nursery. You were thinking about the baby. You whispered Mom's name. You were thinking about her. But me…you've said you won't get rid of me, but that's all. And I get it, I do. You've got a baby coming, and I was just part of the deal with Mom. You can forget me, and you did because when she died, you didn't talk to me about anything. You never even looked at me."

"Emma…" Dan's face is pale. "She'd just died and it wasn't supposed to happen. We had plans, so many plans, and then I saw her die, I saw my wife die and I didn't—Emma, I'm sorry I didn't talk to you, but I do love you. Those aren't just words."

"But they are," I say. "They're just words and that's all they are and I lost two people when Mom died. I lost her and I lost you. Your son will get you and I—" I break off and look at my hands, see how they are knotted together.

"I loved him," I say. "I wanted a brother, I liked picking out nursery stuff, I even wanted Mom to be happier about it, I wanted her to be like us. But then she died and everything became about him. You get up every morning for him, not me, and I…the thing is, I did believe in those words once. In *I love you*. I believed that you did, and that you were—you were my dad. But you stopped being that the day Mom died. You just stopped everything."

I am so tired now. I have said everything inside me, and Dan is just standing there staring at me, and this is what broken is.

I'm so tired. I just want to sleep. I just want to forget, even if it's only for a while, that I saw what I did last night.

That I have told Dan everything and my reply has been silence.

I walk up to my room. I look back once and Dan is still standing in the kitchen. He is still silent.

I don't bother to lock my door when I get to my room. There's no need. There never was. I just wanted to pretend that Dan wanted to come and get me. That I was the one keeping him out when the truth is he was gone from the moment I got to the hospital and said, "What happened?" and Dan said, "Your mother," like he didn't know me.

The whole time, when we sat there and he talked to the doctor and made his choices, during all those terrible hours when she was first gone, he never once looked at me.

40

I wake up to the sun shining in my eyes and it's not like earlier, it's not pretty. I sit up and look at the clock.

It's almost time for Dan and me to be at the hospital. I take a shower, not bothering to wash my hair, and get dressed. As I walk out of my room, I take the padlock off and put it on my dresser. I don't need it.

I just wanted to.

I go downstairs knowing what I will see. I will see a house that is a house and not a home, and I will be alone because Dan and I have said everything and I'm sure he doesn't want to pretend anymore.

The time for pretending ended the second I called him on it.

I take a deep breath.

Everything is out now, everything about what we used to be and what we are now, and I finally get it. I see that this is what Caleb's life is like.

Caleb is alone like I am and he can't fix it but he understands and together we are—together, we are less alone. We are friends. We are—

I think of the noise he made last night when I kissed him, of the warmth of his skin.

We are something that could be.

I will go to the hospital on my own. I'll see Caleb. I…will I even be allowed to see Mom? I don't think Dan would stop that. He's not cruel, he's just gone.

Except he isn't.

He is in the kitchen, still standing where I left him.

"Dan?" I say, and he turns to me, looks at me like he used to, like he did back when I looked at him and saw part of my family.

"I'm sorry," he says. "I'm so sorry," and then he is hugging me and I don't stiffen. I think I will but I don't because I know Dan's hugs and I have missed them. I have missed him.

Words can lie but hugs can't. You know when they are real and this is real and Dan is here and that means he didn't leave me, that he's not going to send me away to Mom's parents or to some boarding school or just kick me out.

It means the Dan I knew is here. That I still matter to him.

"I got lost," he says. "When Lisa died, what you said is true. I've been pretending with you and she was my heart, my world, and she would hate me for how I've acted." He pulls back and looks at me. "I won't leave you again, I swear."

I look at him. I want to believe him. I want to believe him more than anything because everything seems good now but I believed him before too.

"I—all right," he says when I am silent. "I'll prove it. I'll be here. And I'm going to keep being here. But there is one thing you have to know, that you have to hear. I'm not sorry for the choices I made about your mother and brother. I do know it's what she would have wanted. Do you hear me? I *know*."

"No. You believe."

I wait for the withdrawal. The sigh, the words of concern that mean nothing, and the hurt look that will show just that. Just hurt. Nothing past it. Nothing for me.

"Okay, Emma, you have your beliefs and they...they hurt me," he says. "You make it seem like I never loved your mother, and that I somehow chose the baby over her. Do you really believe I don't love your mother? That I wouldn't do anything to have her back?"

I look at him.

"No," I say, and my voice comes out rusty, the word squeezed from me. "I know you loved her. I just—why did she go like that? Why couldn't she have at least said goodbye?"

And then I cry. Dan hugs me again like he used to, like he's really here. Like I matter again. And it's not perfect; it'll never be like it was, there will always be the time I needed him and he wasn't there, and I still can't believe Mom would have ever chosen this silent, frozen life that isn't one. I will always know the fear Dan saw in her wasn't the fear that really was.

I hug him back, though. I don't know if I will ever be able to live with how he shut me out when Mom died, but I do know that Mom loved him. That I loved him.

I know Mom still loves him, because that's who she was.

I don't love him like I did before, but I also know I've missed him even though I wouldn't admit it. I know I've missed how things were.

And I believe he's missed that too. I believe he's missed me.

I believe he wants me around and that makes me feel something I haven't felt in a while.

It makes me feel safe.

41

Mom was not a good storyteller. When I was little, her fairy
tales always got mixed up and forever ended with "And then
some things happened and everyone lived happily ever after.
The end."

"What things?" I'd say and she'd say, "Fairy-tale things,"
and I started asking for stories from books, and I'm not sure
who was more relieved by that, me or her.

Dan was always trying to get her to tell better stories. He
would say, "And then what happened?" when they first started
going out, and even after they got married, even after it was
obvious Mom would say, "Well, then we had a meeting and
there's some stuff that has to be worked out," he kept trying.

And then Mom got involved in this big deal at work and
suddenly she was full of stories. Unfortunately, they were all

about forms and meetings and phone calls, and for weeks Dan and I nodded as she said, "And then I said, 'Tyler, you find that spreadsheet—that's the C one, not the B one—and get me those figures so I can fill out that 5673' and then I took a break and ate an apple and it was one of those awful ones that look great but are all mushy and—"

She kept talking and Dan and I looked at each other and sighed.

"Hey," Mom said. "I saw that. Is my story that boring?"

"Nope," Dan and I said at the same time and Mom said, "You two," and shook her head. "I feel like I'm on the outside here, the person who can't be in the 'tells good stories' group."

Dan and I both said, "No, they're great!"—again at the same time—and Mom laughed and said, "Liars. But I love you both anyway. And this deal is important. The bit about the apple—that, well, okay that not so much."

Dan laughed and I said, "You can't be on the outside."

"You haven't seen you two making faces at my stories," she said.

"No," I said. "I mean, you can't be on the outside because you're everything," and Mom smiled at me and said, "Emma, a family is more than one person. That's why it's a family."

And she was right.

But then again, she usually was.

I can still remember her, pregnant, sitting and watching TV while rubbing her stomach. I actually thought that was normal. But then I realized it wasn't.

I realized too late that she knew our family would change forever.

But now, things might be okay.

She'd like that.

42

When Dan and I get to the hospital, I head for the waiting room.

Dan says, "Thank you," and smiles at me.

I smile back, and who knew a day could be like this, so bad and so good? But then last night was the same too, so awful and then Caleb.

Caleb, who I'm going to see.

But when I step into the waiting room, I see Olivia.

I freeze, and Olivia sees it, I know she does, and it isn't that I don't want to see her or that I wish she was Caleb (although, a small, horrible part of me wishes she was), but that Olivia isn't—

She isn't supposed to be *here*.

Olivia is my link to the me from before. To how things

used to be, and although everything has changed, the one thing that hasn't is us.

"You don't want to see me," she says and she's hurt, I know how her voice wobbles when she's upset, when something's happened that she doesn't want.

"No, it's not—I just didn't think I'd see you," I say, but she gets up to leave, and I see she's done something to her hair after all, put in little braids along the front but they look nice, they have little bows at the bottom and I know Olivia probably wants them to be ironic but they look cute.

"Stop," I say, and she sniffs once and then does, turning her face to the side like she does when she's trying not to cry and this is the thing about her being here: she is so healthy. She is so normal. She doesn't belong here and this is what I didn't want. I didn't want what was left of who I was to disappear.

"When you're here I can't—you're my link to before."

"Before? Oh. You mean before your mom died."

I nod, and she says, "That's why you're always asking me about me, right? Why you only tell me a little about what's going on with you?"

"You know what's going on. My mother's dead and there's a baby."

"But you don't want me here."

"It's not that. It's just that—"

"I'm not Caleb Harrison?"

"What?"

"I'm not stupid," she says. "I've seen you two and now everyone is talking about how you're hanging out with Caleb and you haven't said hardly anything to me about it even though I've asked and asked."

"Olivia—"

"I get it, you're talking to him and you're looking at him and he's looking at you and maybe he gets stuff I don't because of his sister, but do you know how it feels to think that your best friend would rather talk to some guy she barely knows than you? And that I have to hear about it from everyone else! I mean, Anthony tried to talk to me about it. Anthony!"

"I'm sorry, so sorry, but it's not like that. You do know everything, I swear. I just wanted part of my life to not be about *this*." I gesture at the waiting room.

"So when you and Caleb talk, you just talk about your mom?"

She's got me and she knows it, but then, Olivia knows me.

"More than just Mom."

Her eyes fill with tears but she blinks twice, hard. "You weren't in school today. What happened?"

"I saw Dan in the nursery last night. He was putting together a crib and I just—I had to get out of there."

"I know. He called." Olivia folds her arms across her chest, her little braids dancing as she does. "You went out? Caleb?"

"Okay, yes, I saw Caleb last night."

"Don't you want to know how I know? Don't you think he was talking about it in school today?"

"No. I know he wouldn't do that. You know because you know me."

"And you *know* Caleb Harrison well enough to know what

he would or wouldn't say? Are you forgetting this is the guy who drove his dad's car into the lake because he could?"

"No, I know what he's done and yes, I know him," I say, and Olivia sighs.

"All right," she mutters. "I guess you do, because he didn't say anything about you and him to anyone. You really weren't worried?" I shake my head and she sits down. "Why didn't you come see me last night?"

I sit next to her. "Because you really are the only person in my life who's been there for everything. For before Mom died. For after. And you haven't changed. Everything else has, but you haven't, and I don't want..." I swallow. "I don't want you to change. I don't want us to change."

"But we have. Emma, we're still best friends, but when your mom died, everything did change. You've changed. For starters, you're for sure failing all your classes. And then there's Caleb. Don't you think I've seen all of that? What kind of friend would I be if I didn't?"

"Olivia," I say helplessly, and she puts an arm around me.

"You're my best friend," she says. "That hasn't changed. And I get that you need to not talk about your mom and your brother all the time and it's not awful for me to talk about Roger. But you don't have to go to Caleb Harrison to talk about stuff. You never would have done that—"

"Before. I know," I say. "But that's just it, isn't it? That was before, not now. And he—I like him."

"You do remember that he's really messed up, right?"

"Who isn't?" I say, and she looks at me for a moment.

"I want to say something really smart right now, but I got nothing. I hate that."

"You don't need to say something smart. You put up with me. You're here. You've always been here."

"Not *here,* though."

"No," I say. "But now you are. What's it like?"

"Scary. Sad. You do this every day?"

"Yeah," I say, and rest my head on her shoulder. "I like your braids."

"We shouldn't talk about me."

"Why not? I want it to be you and me, not just me. You remind me that life is still out there."

"And Caleb?"

I sit up and look at my hands. "He reminds me of that too, but it's different with him."

"Because he wasn't there before. And because you think he's hot."

"I...yeah," I mutter, scooching down in my chair and she scooches down too, fiddling with the end of one of her braids.

"So you and Caleb?"

"It's—"

"Complicated?"

I nod.

"It's always complicated," Olivia says. "Roger's ex-girlfriend is calling him. It's not like what you're dealing with but—" She picks at one of her braids. "And now I'm talking about myself again."

"And you came here. You're amazing, you know. Roger's ex doesn't stand a chance."

"Amazing?" she says, and I grin at her.

"No, you can't do anything else to your hair."

"Should I leave?"

"No," I say. "Stay."

So she does, until Dan comes and it's time for me to go see Mom.

43

Dan stops me before I go in to see Mom. He says, "Emma?" and I hear *Something's wrong* in his voice.

My stomach twists. I know there is more hurt to come, but I don't know what kind. I sag against the wall and look at him. I wish Caleb was here. I'm glad I talked to Olivia, I am, but Caleb knows what this is like.

"Is it Mom?" I whisper, and Dan shakes his head but slowly, slowly.

"She's—well, the machines are working fine," he says. "Some toxins have built up in her bloodstream but the doctor says that's normal."

He looks at me. "I hate how the doctor talks about her. It's like once I made the choice to—once it was made, Lisa is…

everyone here talks about her like she's here and I catch myself thinking that I need to tell her something or..." He trails off.

I can't do this. I can't say, *No, Dan, you can't talk to her* like I would have because I finally see he gets that she's gone too. I see her and I know she's dead but I still hope and now I know that he does too. I see that someone can be gone and you can still think they will come back.

I see that even when there is no hope, you can still have it.

"Is it very bad?" I say, and it hurts to say it. It really does. The words cut into my throat, slice over my tongue.

"The baby..." Dan says and I tense, thinking of course, *of course,* and he sees that. He takes a deep breath and takes a step back. Says, "You should go see her."

I see how alone he is, and we found a way to reach each other but I can't get there now. I can't forget that Mom walked around holding her stomach and never talked about the baby. I can't forget what I know.

And that's how we part. No words of consolation from either of us. To either of us, and I worry that what we've built will fall apart. I worry nothing will survive, that we all died the morning Mom did.

"Hey," I say when I walk into her room, when I see her. Her face is swollen, and there are more IVs in her arms.

It hurts to look at her.

"I remembered you telling stories," I say. "I miss them. Even the ones about the business deal, the ones Dan and I..." I trail off.

"I found all the food you put away," I tell her. "I found it last night. I...Mom, I drank your bottle of wine." I look at the monitors beeping away. Beeping for her. "I went to see Caleb after that. We slept together. Not like you think, okay? I swear. But I did stay all night and he was so—Mom, I don't get it. I was sure he was glad I was there, even if I did throw up a lot, but I haven't seen him today and I'm scared. I was sure before too, remember? With Anthony. And I was wrong. I just…I just want to know what to do. You knew with Dad and with Dan. How did you know?"

The monitors beep and that's it. That's my reply.

I look at Mom, and she looks so wrong. So…no. I can't think it, even if it is. She's so bloated and her skin is weird-colored and my eyes are burning.

I turn away, but not before I catch a glimpse of her stomach rippling, of the baby turning inside her.

For the first time, I wonder what it's like for him. I see her, but he lives inside her. He lived in her when she was alive. I wonder if he knows the difference.

I wonder if he is scared.

"Hey," I say, and not to Mom. Her belly ripples again and I swallow. I should say something else but I can't. Everything is tangled up inside me, grief and love and hate and worry.

I have never spoken to my brother before.

I close my eyes and keep them closed until Dan comes.

I watch as he kisses Mom goodbye, his lips to hers. I watch him put a hand on her stomach. "Be back soon," he says, and there is no movement under her skin.

No reply.

44

Dan and I walk in silence to the elevator and as we're waiting for it, I hear a familiar sound, a squeaky cart.

Caleb.

I look up, see him and watch him smile at me. Watch the
curve of his mouth, the one I wanted to kiss last night.

The one I still want to kiss, and I fidget, start to look away,
but then remember what he said. That he wanted to kiss me.
That we were together, all night, and granted he spent a lot of
it holding my hair while I puked, but he was there. He helped
me and he held me and when I left I knew I'd see him later.

And so I smile back and it's not like time stops—I don't
have that kind of life anymore because I used to believe that
everything would be okay. That I could have a fairy-tale
perfect life.

I smile back and I'm simply happy to see him.

I believe he's happy to see me, and that's enough.

"Emma?" Dan says, and I look at him, see he's stepped into the elevator.

"Right, coming," I say and just as I get ready to step on, Caleb walks by, brushing a hand against mine and sliding a piece of paper into it.

"You didn't say hi to your friend," Dan says as we get off the elevator, when we're walking out to the car. "Or is he not your friend? I don't know very much about what's going on with you now. I know you see Olivia."

I nod, and I know the note isn't burning my skin. I know that. But it sure feels like it is because I want to read it so bad.

"So, I got a call from your AP History teacher and I also got a letter from the school. What's going on with you and your classes?" Dan says, and I stop and look at him.

"Oh," he says. "That bad?"

"I'm done," I say.

"But you like school so much. Too much, Lisa always says. Said." His voice cracks on that word. "It's different now, isn't it?"

"Yes," I say. "Everything's different now."

Dan's silent as we get into the car and then he says, "So, that guy. Caleb, right?"

I nod.

"Friend? Not friend?"

"Friend."

Dan taps one hand against the steering wheel. "Is he who you were with last night?"

"It's not like that."

"Like what?"

"Like what you're thinking. I feel like I'm taped together most of the time, like I'm a shadow of the Emma that used to be."

"That's when things can happen," he says, and then blows out a breath. "That's what I feel like I should say. But I know what you mean about being taped together and after this morning, I think that what happened last night was important because it made us talk for real. Although I do wish you hadn't gotten drunk."

"Not as much as I do."

"You got sick?"

"More than once."

"What would she do?" he says and I look at the road, my eyes filling with tears.

"I don't—it would be different. None of it would have ever happened."

"Even last night with Caleb?"

I nod.

"Is he like Anthony?"

"*No.*"

"Good. Your mother would be happy about that," Dan says. "I am too. So, he's nice?"

I think about what that question would have meant before, back when my life was grades and planning for the future. When I was so sure I knew what I wanted and I never looked at someone who wasn't in my classes, who didn't have the drive I did, the belief that grades and getting into the best possible college meant everything. When I was that girl, I would have heard the stories—if I ever even noticed him—and believed them, looked through Caleb if I happened to see him. He didn't get what was important, and so he wouldn't have mattered.

I think about what it means now. How I missed so much trying to be the best student. How I could have spent time with Mom and didn't. How I never would have bothered to look past the surface because I was so busy chasing what I thought mattered more. How I thought I could create my future, how I believed I could shape all of it.

I know better now, and Caleb matters to me. He matters to me in a way that's new. That no one else has and it's because he's seen everything, he has seen that I am made up of grief and fury and fear and held a hand out to me. Not to save me, but to just be there.

"He's nice," I say to Dan, who says, "I'm glad, because Anthony—having to listen to him talk when you were doing that debate thing last year—Emma, that boy is an ass."

"He really is," I say, and then we are both laughing but it's a little too loud, a little too hard. A little too brittle.

We have forgotten how to do this normally. We are doing this without Mom and it's weird and we both know it.

But still, we try, and when we get back to the house Dan says, "We're going to be okay."

I look at him, and I can't nod. I can't say yes. But I can say, "I hope so," because it's the truth. Because I can feel myself hoping, and it's scary but it's nice too.

The phone rings and Dan answers it. I head up to my room. I leave the door open.

I sit on my bed and open my hand. I've kept it closed all the way home and my heart is pounding as I look at the piece of paper inside. It's just a note, but it matters.

Caleb matters.

I've never seen his handwriting before. It's cramped, the letters printed, no loops or curls of cursive.

Want to see you, stuck down in recovery handing out magazines. Do you want to come see me tonight? I'm at home if you do.

I fold the note back up and put it in my pocket, walk downstairs and realize I'm tracing over it with one hand, like I can feel Caleb's words through my jeans.

Dan's in the living room, still on the phone. "Remember the Florida thing?" he says to me and then "Hang on," into the phone.

I nod. I remember how he was going to go and talk about what's been done to Mom.

This morning and even the car ride back here suddenly seem very far away and I think again about how Dan never asked me about Mom. I was just her daughter. I just spent my entire life with her. I just love her.

"I've been thinking," Dan says, and I look at him. "I'm not going to go down there."

"You're not?" Does he get it? Does he really finally get it?

"I can't," he says. "You've heard what's going on, and I

can't leave the baby now. I can't leave your mother now. So I'm going to do some teleconference thing with the lawyers. It might be a while, so I was thinking that for dinner—"

He doesn't get it.

"I'm going out," I say.

"Emma, we've talked about this. You know how I feel, and—"

"Yeah, I know, and there's the money for doing it, right?"

"This isn't about the money. At least...we do need it, but I truly believe that if there's a chance another baby can make it and her mother wanted it, then—"

"This mom said that before she died?"

Dan looks away from me. "Her husband knows what she wanted, and I think that a father's wishes count—"

"For everything."

"No, but he should have a say," he says, and I see the moment he gets it, that he remembers what I said to him this morning.

"Emma, I'm sorry. I was in so much pain, and I just wanted to do what your mother wanted, I just wanted to make sure that the baby—"

"I know," I say for what feels like the millionth time, and I am so tired of talking to Dan, of hearing his attempts to make what he's done okay. I'm tired of him pretending he never saw what Mom was really afraid of, that she clutched her belly and kept silent about the baby because she was scared.

I'm tired of him pretending like I got any say in what happened. I'm tired of how he just left me and chose what he wanted. Once that happened, we weren't a family because families talk and he didn't ask me what I wanted. If he had, I—I don't know. I just know I never got to say anything. My voice didn't matter.

Mom knew I was going to get chicken pox before I ever got my first spot. She knew Dan was special as soon as she met him. She knew she loved my dad on their first date. She knew I'd get over Anthony.

I wish I'd spent that last night with her, that I'd put away my books before it was too late and sat with her. That I hadn't been so sure about making the future what I wanted that I forgot the present. That I had a memory of her right before she died besides being at the hospital and hearing she was dead. Before I stood there, alone, and realized I would never see her again.

Before I was told I could see her. That I ended up in this place, this here.

Dan says something as I leave but I don't stop to listen. I have heard it all before and I don't need to hear it again. I don't want this morning and the talk we had poisoned.

I'm afraid it is, though.

I walk and reach into my pocket. I feel the note, Caleb's words, and my heart flutters. Maybe it shouldn't do that, and maybe I shouldn't want it to.

But it does, and I do.

45

Caleb's house looks enormous in the dark, and I shiver a little, not from cold, but from memory of the place, as I head toward it.

He comes down to meet me.

"Hey," I say. "How did you know it was me?"

"I saw you coming," he says. "Not that I was looking for—never mind. I was, you know. Hoping."

I walk over to him. "Have you ever had a day that was good and then bad and then good and then bad and then good again?"

"Your mom?"

"I—" I say and then I'm spilling it all out, how I was happy this morning and then talked to Dan and then things seemed like they would be different but okay, and then we talked again and things were different but not okay. "It felt just like it has since Mom died," I said. "And I—"

"Hoped," Caleb says. "You hoped. I've done that."

"Does it always suck?"

"With my parents it does. But not with everything."

"You're right," I say softly and he is. Hope doesn't always suck because I felt it when I got his note. I felt it walking over here, at the idea of seeing him. I feel it now, when I am with him.

Hope is so simple and so hard to have but it's here, and we have it and it's about each other.

"You wanna come up?" he says, and I nod because I do.

And then, just in case he didn't see, I reach out and take his hand. I've felt it before but now it's not about fear of his house or trying to provide some sort of comfort. It's not a quick brush of fingers, the passing of a note.

I take his hand just to hold it.

His fingers twine with mine and we head up to his room. It's as bare as I remember but smells, strangely enough, like sugar.

"Are you cooking or—?" I say and then break off as I see what's sitting on his counter.

I see a tiny cotton candy machine, like people buy for kids, blue with little animals on it, and beside it are two cones of pink sugar, propped up in a coffee cup.

"Oh," I say because it is all I can say. He did this, he went out and bought a cotton candy machine and made cotton candy, real cotton candy, and it is the sweetest, most amazing thing.

"It's probably cold," he says. "It's not as easy as you'd think to make it and I burned some sugar and it probably smells in here and I'm sorry about that and also, I made three cones but I ate one of them and—"

"Caleb," I say and he stops talking. He stops talking and he looks at me and then he is right there, he is right next to me, in front of me, all around me, and he smells like sugar and I thought I understood want when I was with Anthony that night in the lab but I didn't, it takes you over, your blood, your breath. It is you, it is the world, it is everything, and when his lips touch mine there is nothing but that. But us.

He tastes like sugar, he tastes like Caleb and I want more, I want him. I wrap my arms around him and that's where thought stops. I am all sensation; his breath, the taste of his mouth, his tongue against mine, his lips on my throat, his hair twining around my fingers, his hands on my waist, my hips, and he pulls back, breathing hard, and looks at me like I am—

He looks at me like I am beautiful, and when he does, I am.

"Emma," he says, and he is shaking and I did that to him and I am shaking too and maybe I should be scared but I'm not, I *feel,* and for once it's not anger or sadness or worry it's just want and happiness and I didn't know it could be like this.

Even before, I didn't know.

I pick up one of the cones of cotton candy. He made this for me. I look at him and he is still looking at me as if I'm the only person in the world, as if I'm everything, and as I pick off a piece of cotton candy and eat it, I feel him watching me, I feel him watching my mouth and I hold out the cone, watch him blink at it, watch him sway a little and then grin, take it from my hand.

I watch him eat a piece and I know I am looking at him but I don't care, I want to look at him, at this guy I never saw, who I would have written off and would have never known, and I can't bear the thought of that, of this not happening, and I say, "Caleb," and I hear what is in my voice, all the wonder. All the joy.

He smiles and he is all I can see.

So I kiss him, and the world is just us again and I hope it stays that way forever and ever and ever.

But of course it doesn't.

46

His parents come home. It's hard not to notice, even when you are in the middle of an incredible kiss, because his room shakes and I hear the car.

So does he and we pull apart and look at each other. His lips are redder than usual and his hair is tousled and I did that, I had my hands in his hair.

I was touching him and it's enough to make me forget about the car.

But then another one comes in and the hot light in Caleb's eyes dims and he looks down at the floor as if he can see through it to the garage. To who is in the cars.

"Caleb," I hear, and it's a woman's voice, nice-sounding, sweet-sounding even, and it must be his mother. She doesn't sound like I thought she would, but then I see Caleb's face and remember the house and before I know it I have reached out and taken his hand again.

"I have to go see them," he says. "You don't need to—you shouldn't have to deal with them."

I squeeze his hand gently and say, "I want to."

"I can't," he says, and pulls his hand away. "I can't."

"Oh."

"It's not you," he says. "I know how that sounds, but it's not like that." He looks frantic, frightened.

"So you want me to go?"

He looks at me but doesn't nod. Doesn't say yes. He just stands there.

"Caleb?" I say and his mouth works but nothing comes out. It's like he can't get the words out, like they are too hard, and then he rubs a hand down his face and I see there are tears in his eyes.

"They'll make you hate me," he says. "And if they make you hate me, I don't know what—"

"They can't make me hate you."

"I hate myself when I'm with them," he says, his voice breaking. "So how will you be able to not hate me?"

"Because I know you."

He shakes his head, like it can't be that simple, and says, "No, I—you don't get it."

I step on his foot. Hard. Mom used to do it to Dan when she wanted his attention and he was busy cooking or day-dreaming about some database thing. It seemed to work for her.

"Ouch," he says, and looks at me. Sees me looking at him.

I guess it works for me too.

"I know you," I say again. "And you know me. So trust me."

"Emma," Caleb starts, and I lift my foot up again, lift it up very high. He sees that, and I watch the shadows in his eyes fall back a bit. See the tiniest bit of a smile, fast and fleeting but there, on his face.

"Do you trust me?" he says, low-voiced, and his hands are shaking.

I wonder if he has ever asked anyone else this, and I think he probably has. I think he asked the people who are supposed to love him and I think they said *No*. I think they saw he was breaking and didn't care. I think they let him become broken.

And still he pulled the pieces of who he is together. He is who he is because of who he is and nothing more and that makes him so special.

"I trust you," I say, and look at him. I let what is in my heart out, I let it into my eyes.

I see him look at me. I see him hear what I've said. I see him look into my eyes.

"Emma," he says, and it's too soon to say it, way too soon, but what's in my heart is in his too and he touches my face, cupping the side of my jaw and my name is a prayer in his voice, four letters of joy.

And then we head downstairs. We walk through the garage, which is dark again but warm and filled with the sounds of engines cooling, and then he opens a door to the house.

We walk through it.

47

The house is just like I remember, perfect-looking.

Incredibly sad, a monument to Minnie. It's as if even his parents don't even live here, like this really is a giant, gilded tomb.

Caleb doesn't say anything as we walk through the house but he's holding my hand again and it's shaking a little, damp against my skin.

If you'd told me that I'd be walking hand in hand with Caleb Harrison just a few months ago, I'd have laughed at you. Said, "Who?" probably, and then, "Oh, him. Yeah, sure. That'll happen. And also, everyone will get a magic pony."

But here I am, and there is nowhere else I want to be.

"Hi, Dad," Caleb says, stopping abruptly at the doorway of a room, and I get a glimpse of it over his shoulder. It's one of the ones he showed me, filled with untouched-looking furniture and a portrait of Minnie hanging on the wall with all the lights in the room shining on it.

His father says something. It might be "Hello," but it might just be a grunt. He's looking through a folder of papers with one hand, a glass more than half-full of amber liquid in another. I don't need to wonder what it is. I can smell the alcohol from here.

"Caleb," someone else says. I see his mother stepping out of a dim corner of the room, stepping away from a chair covered with files. He does have her hair, but where his is free, wild and curly and falling all over the place, hers is pulled back into a tight knot with exactly two strands allowed loose, curling over her ears and down along her face.

"Hi, Mom," he says. "How was work?"

"Fine," she says, and the way she's looking at him is—it's like he's some sort of animal that she's forced to see and doesn't want to.

She hates him for living. I see that, and the force of that hate makes me want to cry.

I can't even imagine how it makes Caleb feel.

"Do you need something?" she says, and she's so polite, but it's the kind of polite you are to someone you know you have to see but don't want to. The kind that is all surface.

She blinks, glancing at me, and for a moment, I see who she really is under the icy layers, the hate. I see pain so deep it's endless.

I see that she is broken too, and that she blames Caleb for it.

"No," Caleb says, and his hand is really sweating in mine

now, and he's holding on tight, holding on as if I am keeping him standing upright. "I just heard you call when you came in. I'll go now."

His mother doesn't say a word, just shrugs, and I watch her eyes fall on Minnie's portrait as if they have to, as if it is the only thing she can see. I watch her face relax, soften.

I realize Caleb is no longer around. Not in her mind. She saw him just now, but she didn't, not really. I bet she hasn't seen him since the night Minnie died.

I knew grief could destroy you, but I didn't know it could turn you into the walking dead. A shiver crawls up my spine because there is something in her blankness and hatred I understand. Something I see in myself.

It would be so easy for me to make my entire life about Mom, about what happened to her. It would be so easy for my whole life to be hating Dan. Hating the baby.

Caleb feels my shudder because he glances at me and then starts to turn away, starts to walk us away from his parents.

"It's polite to introduce your guests," his father says, and his voice is falsely chipper, laced with something bitter.

"I—sorry," Caleb says. "Mom, Dad, this is Emma."

"Emma," his father says, and drains the rest of his glass. "Very nice to meet you."

He doesn't look at me when he says it.

"Emma?" his mother says, turning away from the picture of Minnie, and her gaze is so needy and empty and angry and lonely it actually hurts to see it. "Wait, I know that name. You're that girl, aren't you? The one whose mother died."

Caleb's hand suddenly clamps down hard on mine and it's

not just his fingers that are shaking now. He's shaking all over, trembling so hard I can feel it, and I get why just as she says, "There was something else too…a baby?"

"Yes," I manage to get out, and Caleb's father says, "Are you the girl whose father is keeping the body alive for the baby?"

"Stepfather, and yes," I say again, and he looks at me as if he didn't expect me to speak.

"I'm sorry," Caleb's mother says, and her voice is very stiff and very brittle, but I think she means it. "I know how painful loss can be."

She looks at Caleb, and her gaze changes. So does her voice. "When did you meet my son?"

"We go to school together."

His father looks at me now. "And you started talking after her mother died?"

"I—" I say, and then realize he isn't talking to me. He's talking to Caleb.

"Yes," Caleb says, low-voiced. "We started talking then."

"Of course you would. First the drugs, then the cars, but you will not hurt another girl. Do you understand me? You. Will. Not."

He looks at me then.

"You need to leave," Caleb's father says, and he sounds normal. But the light in his eyes isn't.

"Yes," his mother says. "Go right now. You don't—" She makes a low, keening noise. "You don't want to get hurt, do you?"

They want me to go. No, more than that. They mean I should go and leave Caleb. They—

I think they think they are saving me in their own icy, twisted way.

They think he could hurt me.

That he would.

Caleb, staring at the floor, starts to let go of my hand but I won't do it. I hold on.

I hold on and look at him until he feels my gaze. I look at him until he looks at me and then I say, "I'm happy to go, but I want Caleb to come with me. It's dark out, you know, and I'd feel better if he could walk me home. I know I'm safe with him."

His mother starts to say something but then stops and turns back to the picture of Minnie as if I'm no longer there at all.

His father doesn't look away, though. He closes his folder and says, "Has he told you that he hit someone? That he stole a car and then ran someone down? That was at night. So I don't know how safe you'd be with him. His own sister certainly wasn't."

I can't believe this. I can't believe *them*. How they talk to him. How they treat him.

How they don't see who he is at all. I take a deep breath.

"I know he hit someone because he told me. And Minnie? I think she was safe with him. She knew she was supposed to wear a helmet when she rode her bike but somehow you can't see that. Caleb did his best and all you do is blame him for it," I say. "And me? I *know* I'm safe with Caleb."

His father shakes his head and gets up. He walks out of the

room, careful not to touch either Caleb or me. His mother stays where she is, but she is looking at me as if I've spoken a foreign language.

And for a second—just a second—I think she hears me.

But then she goes back to the dark corner. To her chair, where I realize she can look up and see only Minnie's portrait.

Caleb doesn't move. He just stands there and I turn to him, worried about what I'll see.

He looks upset, but he also looks surprised, and when I start to walk away, ready to get out of this house, he follows, his hand still in mine.

"Emma," he says as we approach the door and then he puts his arms around me, right there in that frozen house. He's shaking, hard, and I realize that part of him still believed he killed Minnie, that even though he told himself it wasn't true, that even when he tried to live as if it wasn't, there was a part that screamed it was.

There are other things he's done, things he will have to live with, and there is no perfect ever-after coming for him, but I swear I can actually feel some of the anger and grief he carries flowing away, flowing out of him.

It lasts for a second, maybe two, but that's enough. I can tell because when he whispers, "Let's get out of here," I know it's because he wants to and not because he has to.

Maybe that one word—*wants*—doesn't seem like much of a difference.

But it is.

"You believe in me," he says when we're outside, out on the street and this dark is so much warmer than that house.

"You trust me." He touches my hair, my face, and then kisses me once, gently.

"Not enough," he murmurs, and kisses me again, kisses me harder, and I smile, open my arms to him, myself to him, and we stand there in the darkness, in its embrace, its warmth and fall into each other.

It's so much. It's everything.

It's late, after midnight, when my stomach rumbles and his does too and we go and get burgers, eat them in the parking lot after walking through the drive-through and laughing at the looks we get, and we are still kissing. In between bites of burger and sips of soda we are kissing like we can't stop.

He pulls away, breathing hard, and says, "This is crazy."

"Yes."

"But right."

"Yes," I say again and we grin at each other. He looks at me, right at me, in that way he has, like he sees all the way inside me and what he sees is beautiful, and I close my eyes because I don't want this moment to end. I like being happy.

It's nice, and I don't think I ever enjoyed it like I should have.

I didn't know happiness could be lost, but it can be.

"Emma, are you—?" He pauses. "You should go home, right? Talk to Dan about everything again."

"It's not my home," I say, and it hasn't been, not since Mom died, but I want it to be. I want that house to be my home again, I want it to be more than a place where I sleep, where memories coil around me and dig their way under my skin, leaving space for grief's thorns to burrow deeper still.

I want things to be right again and I thought they could be today and then I realized they couldn't and I still—

I still have to go back.

I still have to see Dan. And I do have to talk to him again. Not for him. Not even for Mom. But for me.

"You're right. I do need to talk to Dan."

It feels strange to say that. I don't know when I last said that and meant it.

It feels strange but not false. It feels true, and that's because it is. Because life has come and changed things. Changed Dan, changed me, and maybe grief is all we will share. Maybe it's all we will ever share now and will break the family we were into nothing.

But I should know. I need to know.

So Caleb walks me back to the house. Home. That word still feels false when I think it. Feels false when I look at where I live. At where I once took everything inside for granted.

I kiss Caleb before I walk up the driveway, but I don't say goodbye. I've had enough of that word forever. I don't want to have to say it again. Not for a very, very long time.

"Emma," he says, and I look back at him. Watch him walk toward me, and he is the trifecta, like Olivia said. He is beautiful, but the thing that truly makes him so is on the inside.

Is his heart, and I touch his chest, feel it beat against my hand.

It beats fast but sure. Solid. I like that.

"See you tomorrow. Well, today," he says, and then he kisses me again. His heart beats faster when our lips meet.

"Hi," he says when we separate, and smiles at me. He understands what it's like to not want to say goodbye too.

And this—all of this, everything that's happened between us—it feels like something. It is something.

It's a beginning.

"Hi," I whisper back and then turn away and walk to the house. I look back once, because I know it's important to do that now. To see the people that are in your heart.

He's there, and he waves. I wave back and then go forward.

The kitchen light is on and I see Dan standing by the stove like he's waiting for me.

Maybe he needs to do this too, to figure out if what we were can be somehow saved or if we have to let it all go.

I walk into the house. I walk into the kitchen.

"Dan," I say, and he looks at me.

He looks at me and I know something is wrong. Horribly wrong.

"There's been—" he says and his voice is thick with tears. "There's a problem, and this time I want to talk to you about it. I want to know what you think we should do."

48

I almost say, *Mom?*

In spite of everything, I almost say it. I almost ask *What's happened to her?* even though nothing can happen to her now.

Over a month of her being gone and I still see her.

Every day, I see her.

I've hated Dan for making his choice without asking me, for holding Mom's body here for the baby.

But what I hate him for most of all is that he's made it so I can see her. So that I can sit with her, touch her, watch her chest rise and fall. Every day, I see her breathe and tell myself she's dead. I tell myself she's gone, that she left the moment a blood vessel in her brain burst without warning.

I tell myself she's dead.

I have told myself that all along, but part of me doesn't believe it.

I didn't see her die. I didn't see her fall to the ground. I didn't see her leave.

I never even saw her body. Not until after Dan had made his choice. Not until after machines made her heart beat again, made her lungs breathe again, made her body here again.

Not until after I could sit with her. Hold her hand. Rest my head on her shoulder.

Be with her.

I know all that's left is her body, but there's so much power in that, in seeing the face and hands and hair of my mother. I know that there's a place machines can't reach, that there is no way to hold on to who a person is when they die, no way to capture what makes them who they are and keep it with you.

You can hold on to their body, but not them. Who they are slips away. Flies free.

But it's hard to remember that when you see someone you love. When you can touch them, talk to them, hold their hand.

I have hated Dan for choosing the baby, for keeping Mom's body alive.

I have hated him for making me hope when I know there isn't any.

I hate him for what he's done to Mom, but I hate him just as much for what he's done to me.

So I almost say, *Mom?* and as the word bubbles scorching up my throat I feel my hands knot into fists because it isn't her, it can't be her, he can't be talking about her, and yet here I am almost asking. Hoping.

This is what it all comes back to. To what happened, and how I never got a chance to say goodbye. I never got a chance to say anything.

Dan made his choice. He picked the baby without any thought, without even asking me what I thought. It was like I didn't exist in that moment and now Mom's body beats and breathes for it. Her body exists and I can see it. I can see her. I have seen her.

But it isn't her at all.

"It's not your mother," Dan says, seeing my face, my clenched fists, and I think of how Caleb must have felt when he came home from his summer away and saw his parents looking at him just like they had when his sister died. How empty he must have felt.

How furious.

"I know it's not her. She's dead."

Dan flinches. "I know she's dead too," and he saw what I didn't. He saw Mom—my mother, God, my mother—he saw her life end. He saw her stop breathing. He was there when she left. He got to say goodbye like I haven't.

I was happy—just now, I was happy. I know I was. I can remember it, being happy just now with Caleb.

How can it be gone so fast? How can life be so cold?

How could it take Mom away from me?

I want my mother. I had her for seventeen years, but I thought I had forever. I thought I was ready for anything, I had my whole life planned, but seventeen years is nothing when it's gone in the time it takes someone to reach for a piece of toast.

It's nothing when the one person you were sure would be there, would always be there, is gone.

I sink to the floor now, weightless, boneless. I wait to cry but the tears won't come. They have always come before. I have cried more than I ever thought I could, oceans of tears since the day she died and I first saw her again.

But I can't cry now. I want to, but grief has wrapped itself around me so tight that there's nothing left. Its thorns have closed around me, burrowed all the way inside. Grief has found the tiny thread of hope I held on to in spite of everything and snipped it, pinned it with a thorn to my still-beating heart.

Dan isn't going to talk to me about Mom. He is alive. I am alive.

She isn't.

"Emma?" Dan says, and he is kneeling next to me now. I can feel him looking at me. I can hear him breathing, and here we are exactly where I thought we'd never be. I was going to finish school and leave.

I wasn't going to be left.

"I hate you," I say, and the words come out as flat and empty as I am, and Dan sits down across from me.

"I know," he says, and his voice is as flat as mine too. As empty. "But I meant what I said when you came in. I didn't ask you what to do about your mother before, but I'll ask you now. It's—it's the baby, Emma."

The baby.

I stare at him.

"It's his heartbeat," Dan says softly. "There are problems. It's not strong enough, not all the time. The doctor says there's a chance he can make it to forty-three days, to the twenty-five week mark, but if his heartbeat doesn't stabilize he might die. And all the doctor says is that there's a chance he'll make it. That's all he'll say. That there's a chance and—" He breaks off and then grabs my hands. His fingers are cold and shaking so hard I feel their tremors rattling across my palms, up my arms.

"What do I do?" he says. "Do I let the doctors deliver him now, even though he'll almost never make it, or do I wait and hope that he'll make it to forty-three days? I already know he'll never see his mother. I don't—the thought Emma, of him never seeing me or you…" He squeezes my hands tight, and now my hands are cold too.

So cold, and he says, "What should I do?"

I look at him and he is looking back at me and he doesn't know what to do, he is scared and lost and the baby could die, his heart could stop beating just like Mom's did.

One heartbeat, two heartbeats, three heartbeats, more, and you never know when you have used yours up.

That's the thing. You don't know.

How long will your heart beat for? How many heartbeats do you have?

I look at Dan and see he is waiting for my answer. That he needs me. That he wants me to help him. To be with him.

To be his family.

But I don't know what to say.

49

I don't know what to say but I do. That's the thing.

I do.

It has always been about Dan and what he wants. It has always been about the baby.

He's kept Mom's body alive for the baby, kept her lying in a hospital bed, here but not here.

Let her go, I told him when I finally knew, when it was too late, and that's all I need to say now.

Let her go.

Let *him* go.

Let it all go.

I pull away from Dan and stand up.

I just have to say it. I just have to say *Let go. Let her go.*

Let them go.

"Emma?" Dan says, "Emma, please talk to me," but I'm not listening to him. I don't want to even hear him.

I step into the living room. I used to sit with Mom on the sofa. Right here, right where I am sitting down now. I should have sat with her more. Been with her more.

I wish I had, but I didn't. I only sat with her when I thought I could, when my "schedule" would allow it.

"Emma," Dan says again, pleading now, and I shake my head.

I didn't spend enough time with Mom. I thought I would see her get old and even worried about it once in a while, about what would happen to her, vague thready thoughts about how I would manage my life and take care of her and Dan when they were old.

I worried about the future and I waited for it too. I wanted Mom to see me do all the things I'd planned.

I thought it would matter if I was first in my class, if I got into a school that made people jealous, if I had a GPA that was so high no one else could reach it.

I was going to talk about dedication when I was valedictorian, planned on standing on stage and talking about how I wanted to follow in my father's footsteps, about how I knew I was making my mother proud.

I'd planned all that and it's too late to go back, too late to take back all those nights I worked for extra credit I never needed, the nights I spent preparing for tests I was already prepared for.

It's too late to take them back and to just sit with her on this sofa. Be with her.

She's gone, and I sat beside her a few nights before she died, desperate to get to my homework, but she'd had a bad day at work, lots of phone calls that left her upset and tense, and she just wanted me to watch TV with her for a while, said, "Come on, sit and rest for a minute. If I can do it, you can do it. Right?"

I remember it so clearly. I didn't want to, mumbled and muttered about homework but sat down, and she'd sighed and put her feet up on the coffee table.

They were swollen.

I'd forgotten that until now.

I remember that I could see the marks her shoes had left, and said, "Mom, you need new shoes."

"No, it's just the baby," she'd said. "It's what happens."

"Your feet must hurt," I'd said, and stopped thinking about homework and focused on her.

I wish I'd done that more now.

"A little," she'd said, wiggling her toes, and flipped through the channels. She'd stopped on a sitcom we'd both seen a million times before, four friends living in "the big city" and trying to "make their way in the world." They would, of course. That's the beauty of TV. Everything works out in the end.

Mom had flipped through the channels during a commercial and now I lean into the sofa, lean into where she was sitting, and remember her doing that.

I remember it all because I was really and truly there with her then.

I noticed.

I saw her holding the remote. I saw images flickering by

one after another. An infomercial, a bad movie, an okay movie, an ad, another comedy, more ads.

She stopped on an ad for a restaurant.

I remember thinking that was weird because it was a restaurant ad and who hadn't seen one? We'd just seen ten alone, but the ad she watched—

There was a family sitting in a booth, smiling as the waitress dropped off their enormous platters of food.

"Are you hungry?" I'd said, thinking of how Mom had eaten all of her dinner and then gone back to the fridge to make a sandwich, Dan trying to help and her saying, "I'm pregnant, Dan. I can handle bread. Look, here I am holding one slice! And now another! Next thing you know, I'll be able to pick up mustard all by myself! Amazing, isn't it?"

"No," Mom had said to me as I asked her about the ad she'd stopped on, and her voice was quiet, so quiet. "I'm not hungry."

"Are you sure?"

"I'm sure."

I looked at her because I wasn't sure—she was eating a lot and still had a bit of mustard on her chin—and she was staring at the TV.

She was staring at the ad, at the food on the table, at the waitress smiling.

At the family. The mother, the father, the daughter and the baby in the high chair reaching for the "grown-up" food and making everyone laugh.

Special Deal! flashed across the screen and Mom sighed and put a hand on her belly. On the tiny rise that was there.

"We'll do that," she whispered. "We'll do that."

"Not there," I said. "Dan hates that place."

She smiled and said, "He does, doesn't he? But we'll all go somewhere nice and it'll be just like that ad."

I hurt. I actually hurt all over, and I see what I missed and I can't stop it even though I want to.

I remember how she touched her stomach again, stroking over the tiny bump. She whispered, "Do you hear that, baby? We'll do it. We will. You just hang in there for me. You stay with me."

"Where's he going to go?" I said, and then "Can we go back to the show?" and she said, "Sure," and we did, we went back to the sitcom and that was it.

Except it wasn't.

I thought I knew what she wanted, but I didn't.

She wanted that picture the ad showed; she wanted that family—the mother, the father, the daughter, the baby. She wanted all of us together, and when I saw her touching her stomach I thought she was hungry and then, later—*after*—scared.

And she was scared, but not like I thought. Not for herself.

She didn't want to be kept still. She didn't want bed rest.

But she did it.

She did it because she wanted the baby to be here. She wanted the baby to be here and all those times I heard her crying when she wasn't pregnant or when she miscarried were because she was in pain.

But also because she wasn't pregnant.

She wanted what she saw in that ad that night I thought

I was being with her. She wanted something so simple. She wanted all of us to be together. She wanted me and Dan and the baby and her together forever and ever.

She gave up so much to get pregnant and the thing is—

The thing is she *wanted* it. She wanted him, the baby swimming inside her. I thought she was scared and she was, but not of him.

She was scared for him.

She agreed to bed rest, terrified of it, for him.

She wasn't afraid of dying.

She was afraid *he* would.

I see her now, really see her, and all the moments I thought Mom was scared for herself, all those moments where she touched her stomach and I saw fear in her eyes I thought I knew what it was for. I thought she knew what was coming and didn't know how to escape it.

I was wrong.

She touched her stomach because she wanted to know the baby was there. Because she wanted to feel him. Because she wanted him to stay with her. She didn't talk about names because she was afraid to pick one, afraid she'd lose him like all the other babies she'd almost had, and those hadn't swum inside her for nearly as long, those hadn't lived long enough for names to even be an issue. She'd wanted him to make it. To be with her and me and Dan.

She'd wanted him to live.

Mom, I think, *Mom,* but I am just a girl on a sofa, a girl whose mother woke up one morning and died because that's how life is.

I hurt all over even more now, like someone has shattered my insides, like I've been torn apart and put back together but I'm missing something.

Her.

And him. My brother.

I know that, and I know what I need to do. What Mom would want me to.

A family is more than one person.

"Dan," I say, and wait till he turns toward me.

50

I'm at the hospital. I'm just...I'm just standing in a corner of a hall on one of the floors.

It's small. Quiet. It's where I want to be. Where I need to be.

It's been forty-three days since Mom died, and I'm finally going to do it.

I'm finally going to say goodbye.

"I'm sorry," I say as I sit down and take her hand, which is cool and almost papery. I can't bring myself to look at the rest of her. I want to remember the way she was before all this happened. "I'm so sorry I didn't see that you wanted the baby so badly. That you weren't scared about yourself at all. I wish I'd spent more time with you. I wish—" My voice cracks. I lace my fingers through hers, tears welling as I have to move her fingers to make it happen. "I wish you were here but you aren't. I miss you, Mom. I miss you and I know I always will but…" I bite my lip hard and make myself keep talking. "But today everything changes. And even though you aren't here, I know you're happy. That you'll be happy with what's going to happen. With how things are going to be."

I let my fingers fall away from hers, catch her hand and put it gently by her side. "I love you. I miss you." I start to cry. I can't tell her goodbye. She's still with me. She'll be with me forever. I love her that much and she loved me that much too.

I sit there with her for a little while longer, until I'm not crying. Until I can look at her stomach.

She's twenty-five weeks pregnant now.

Forty-three days, and the baby's heart is still beating.

In fact, he'll be born today. Dan and I picked out his name together.

Liam.

And now, the operation to bring him here has started. Dan wasn't sure how long it would last. The doctors—there are more of them now, more of them here for this moment—aren't even sure.

Liam won't come into the world like most babies do. Mom's body will be there, but she won't, and when he comes out she'll be—that will be it. He'll have to be taken to ICU right away.

I blow out a breath as I think of what will happen.

The machines that have kept Mom's heart pumping, her lungs breathing, will be turned off. Her body will be empty. Silent.

Liam will never hear her breathe on her own. Never touch her for real. Left unsaid is what might happen to him. Left unsaid is that no one has been able to say if he will ever draw his first breath.

Left unsaid is that he might slip away like Mom did. That he could be here. And then be gone.

"We don't know what will happen," the doctor who will head the operation told Dan and me last night. "We think things look good, but—"

I stopped listening then. I held Dan's hand.

He held mine back and when we got home we looked at the photos of Mom we've been collecting. They are for Liam. They are for us.

I am still in the corner where I stood before I said goodbye to Mom when Caleb rubs my arm gently. He's been with me since I got to the hospital, walked with me to this corner and stood, waiting, for me to come back. He came to be with me.

Olivia came over this morning. She brought doughnuts but no one ate them. We just sat there, around the table, talking about Mom. Dan told us how she used to call him at home from work and ask him what he was making for dinner, sighing and saying, "If I'd known getting married would mean dinner every night, I would have done it years ago."

Olivia told us about how she'd managed to get her parents to agree to stay home and meet Roger, who had not only told his ex to stop calling him but, when she came up to him at a party when he was with Olivia and acted like she wasn't there, said, "This is my girlfriend, Olivia," which was pretty much perfect boy behavior and Olivia figured after that, her parents would be easy.

"I told them they needed to talk to him without any gadgets the whole time. I figure I've got two minutes, tops, but still, I want them to meet him." As soon as she said it, she added, "But if you need me—"

"I do," I said. "I'll need you when I get home and tomorrow and for the rest of my life. I also know I need you to be happy. And besides, it's not like I'm not going to tell you everything anyway."

"Promise?"

I gave her a look and she grinned, but still hugged me before we left and whispered, "Emma, I'm here if you need anything. You know that, right? You can even call my mom or dad if it's an emergency."

That was big stuff and I hugged her because she was awesome and I knew she meant everything and because Olivia has been here through it all and she has always been my friend. Mom would call her "a keeper."

Mom's right. But like I always knew—she usually was.

Olivia and I are fine, and she is going to have her parents meet Roger, just like she's finally starting to be okay about me and Caleb.

"I know you," she said to me last week, "and you're happy when you're with him. Really happy and it's been a while. So I'm happy. I just...I mean, you, Miss I-Have-To-Be-Perfect and a car thief. I never would have guessed."

"Me either," I said, and it was true. The me I was before never would have guessed. Never would have seen.

But I—the me I am now—I do see. And I am happy with Caleb.

Caleb.

When I told him what I'd said to Dan, that I wanted to go ahead and do the very thing I'd been fighting against, that I wanted to keep Mom's body beating and breathing so that Liam might live, he didn't say anything. He just held me and I cried.

I cried because I was happy and scared and still a little angry. I am all those things still and Caleb was there. Is here.

We are together. We walk with each other when we can between classes in school. We talk when we can. He even eats lunch with me and Olivia. People have said stuff, but he doesn't care and the girl I used to be, the girl who would have, is gone. I am not going to be valedictorian, I'm not going to even be in the top twenty. I'm probably going to summer school to make up a bunch of my classes. (Okay, I'm definitely going, and Dan has started homework checks, which are weird, but I get why he's doing it).

In the end, it's okay because now I walk through school and see that it isn't everything. That it's just a part of my life and that it shouldn't be everything.

I know what matters.

Caleb does too.

When he kisses me, I am still here, I am still in this life, in my life, but I am glad to be there. Glad to be the me who saw him. Who gets to hold him.

Things haven't changed for him. His parents are the same, and they won't change. That's another thing about life I've learned. The people who need to see things clearly the most tend to miss life, believe they are living it when they are only letting it pass by.

Caleb still hurts in a way I understand, but not because of them. He hurts for his sister. That's how grief is.

Grief holds you tight. It holds you forever.

But we can hold each other too, and we do. I know he is thinking of me and Minnie, just as I am thinking of him and Mom.

"Should we go?" he says after a while, after it's been—after we both know enough time has almost passed, and I nod.

This is the part of grief that hurts the most.

"She was the best mother," I tell him. "Fun. Strong. She loved me. She loved Dan. She loved…she loved Liam. I miss her so much."

Beside me, Caleb lets out a deep, shuddering breath. When he speaks, his voice is very low, just above a whisper.

"I miss Minnie," he says. "I miss her waking up before everyone else and making so much noise we all got up too. I miss her coming into my room and going through my stuff. I miss her asking me to make her chocolate milk. I never realized how quiet—it's so quiet in the house now, you know?"

We should go, but neither of us do. We are both thinking of people we love. Of people we have lost. Of people who left us before we thought they would.

But we are here.

We are here, and we walk to the elevator together. Caleb kisses me while we wait for it.

"Hi," he says, and I smile at him, touch his hair, parting his curls so I can see his eyes.

"Hi," I say, and then whisper, "I'm scared." I thought saying it out loud would make it—I didn't think it would make it disappear, but I thought it would make it easier.

It doesn't.

"I know," Caleb says, and we get off the elevator, walk to the waiting room. We sit, two people among others whose faces are creased with worry too, and flip through old magazines.

We sit and wait and when I have looked through all the magazines he buys me chips and a soda, kisses me when I ask what time it is because I just asked before he went to the vending machines.

He kisses me and for that kiss, for that moment, I forget how worried I am. It comes back, of course, but with Caleb, I feel more whole—I am more whole—than I have been since Mom died.

I love him.

I love him because of who he is, who he really is past what everyone else sees—the lost boy, the druggie, the car thief. I love him because he is strong and caring. I love him because he broke and put himself back together again. I love him because he is beautiful inside and out.

I love him for being here with me. I love him for not telling me that everything will be all right. I love him because he knows what life is like, what it can do, and is always honest about it.

"Caleb," I say, and he looks at me. Smiles.

"I love you," he says, and that is how it is. How we are. He knows I love him without me saying it, just like I know he loves me.

But I do like it when he says it. I glow inside when he does.

"I love you too," I say, and I had no idea he'd come into my life. That being with him—loving him—could be so right. But it is. We are.

I love you is just words but it is more than that when you mean them. When you feel them.

So yes, I love him, he loves me, and it matters. It matters a lot, but there is still no news and I knot my hands together, squeeze.

No news and no Dan, who I last saw getting ready to go back to be with Mom and Liam for the operation. Who said, "You can still come."

But I couldn't. I had to talk to Mom for one last time, and I did.

She's gone, but I can be happy. I can be in love. I can be both those things and scared too, and I am. I am, and this is what life is.

I sit next to Caleb, waiting and thinking about what life really is. About how it has its own will. How it shows you things that rip you open, tear your world apart. How it unfolds even when you think it can't. How it takes you places you never thought you'd be. Shows you things you never knew you wanted to see. Brings you pain—and joy.

Where will it take me now?

I don't know. And that's what life is. You can plan all you

want, but you will never know what will be. Life just is, and I am here in it. I am waiting for what comes next.

I hear a noise, footsteps, and Caleb says, "Emma," wonder in his voice.

I look and I see Dan.

I see Dan, and he is smiling. He is gesturing, hands flying, and I know I have a brother. That Liam is here, he's made it, and when I can, when the doctors will let me, I will fly to the ICU to see him. To tell him all the things we will do together. To wait to be able to hold him for the first time.

I will always carry Mom in my heart. I will always miss her. I will always wish she was here.

I will always know what life can take, but I am ready to see what it can give.

I'm ready to move forward.

★ ★ ★ ★ ★

ACKNOWLEDGMENTS

A very special thank you to Natashya Wilson and everyone at Harlequin Teen for their enthusiasm, encouragement and general all-around awesomeness.

Robin, Beth, Diana and Jess—thank you for all your support, kindness and for, well, being who you are.

Thanks also go out to the following fantastic members of my mailing list: Sebrina Parker Schultz, Petra (Safari Poet), Samantha Page Townsend, Nicole Hackett, Autumn Nelson, Renee Combs, Alexandria, Tess Puhak, Ashley Evans, Christi Aldellizzi, Nakoya Wilson, Hannah Joy Herring, Stephanie Fleischer, Meghan Dondero, Nancy Woodford, Lexi Welch, Genevieve Swords, Lauren Becker, and Lucile Ogie-Kristianson.

A special shout-out to Christi Aldellizzi for not just being a mailing list star, but for being so generous in giving to help out victims of Hurricane Sandy. Christi is another reason I know that my readers are the BEST readers ever.

Lastly, thank you to all the librarians, booksellers and readers who talk up my books. Your support means so much to me!

DISCUSSION QUESTIONS

1. *Heartbeat* explores a relatively rare situation in which Emma's mother is dead but her body is being kept alive due to her pregnancy. What did you think about the situation? How did grief affect Emma's actions and feelings?

2. What do you think Emma would have done if Dan had made her part of the decision when her mother died?

3. Olivia is Emma's sole friend when the story begins. Why do you think Olivia stays by Emma's side throughout her grief and changing attitudes? What do you think makes a friendship strong?

4. Caleb and Emma are brought together initially through cir-

cumstance and then shared grief. Do you believe their relationship has a chance to last and grow? Why or why not?

5. Why did Emma fear that Dan might choose to send her away? What was at the root of her fears?

6. Emma's attitude toward school undergoes a 180-degree change before and after her mother's death. What do you think will happen with her attitude in the future and why?

7. *Heartbeat* explores Emma's journey from grief to hope through different kinds of love—family love, friendship, and romantic love. How did each type affect Emma? What helped her, and did any hinder her? What do you think Emma will pass on to her baby brother as he grows up?

Q & A with Elizabeth Scott

Q: Tell us a little about yourself and how you came to be an author.

A: *I fell into writing fiction by total accident. When I was in school, I went out of my way to avoid any "creative" writing assignments because I didn't think I had any imagination. Also, all the writers I knew seemed very intense and talked a lot about "the craft," and it seemed kind of scary. I just wanted to read books, not write them!*

I wrote what ended up being my first piece of fiction while I was at work, bored out of my mind in a meeting, and I wasn't intense and certainly didn't know anything about writing, but I did learn one thing—writing stories was fun! I joined an online critique group and never looked back after that. I think the thing I love about writing the most, besides getting to tell stories, is that there's always more to learn. There are always new things to try and hopefully, ways to be better!

Q: What inspired you to write *Heartbeat*?

A: *I'd read a newspaper article about the death of a pregnant woman and thought, "What if she'd died but the baby hadn't?" It turns out that once in a while, that does happen, and the moment I learned that, Emma sprang into my head.*

Q: Emma and Olivia have a strong friendship. What do you think is important in a friend?

A: *Someone who gets you. It might not sound like much, but everyone has a messy/dark side, and my friends, the ones who have been in my life for a long time—they get it. And they're okay with it.*

Q: What kind of research did you do while writing *Heartbeat*?

A: *Obviously, there's not a lot out there about Emma's situation, but I read about premature births and prenatal care. And I'd read several books about the "camp" Caleb mentions being sent to and knew I wanted him to have been to one.*

Q: As an author, you probably like many of your characters, but tell us, do you have a secret favorite?

A: *I don't, because I can't read my books! I mean, if I have to do a reading, I'll pick out a passage, but that's it. So many writers I know can read their own stuff once it's published, but I can't. I've tried a couple of times, but have yet to make it past the first few pages. I guess I'd rather just be writing something new!*

Q: What do you hope that readers will remember after finishing *Heartbeat?*

A: *Honestly, I just hope they like it! I'm not a big fan of "message" books. I just want to tell a story and if people like it, then YAY!*

Q: What advice do you have for aspiring authors?

A: *Read. I meet so many people who want to be writers, who have written stories/novels, and when I ask them what they last read, they just look at me. I was a reader long before I became a writer and I think that if you don't love reading, then why are you writing? Also, don't just read what genre you write. Read everything you can get your hands on. Read stuff that you wish you could write. (In my case, it's poetry.)*

Thank you, Elizabeth!

*Turn the page for an exclusive look at the next
powerful and romantic contemporary novel
from award-winning author Elizabeth Scott*
HOPE LIES

I was eating peas when the police came for my mother.

"Warren?" my mother said when the doorbell rang. She didn't like interruptions during dinner, but they still happened sometimes. And they were always for my father, who could never quite leave work, even when he wasn't in the office.

Dad got up, giving my mother a rueful smile, then shooting a longing glance at his roast beef as he left the room.

"Victoria," he called out a moment later, his voice strangely tense, and my mother, frowning slightly, put her fork down and got up.

"I bet it's the club," I said. The Pleasantfield Country Club was always trying to get my parents to donate money, even though the only time they did was for charity fund-raisers.

"Eat your peas, Isabel," my mother said as she left the dining room. I guiltily rolled them out from under the pile of what I'd thought were artfully arranged meat scraps.

As soon as she left though, I picked up my plate and dumped as many as I could onto my father's. It wasn't a big deal. He liked peas.

Dad came back as I was putting my plate down. He looked strange, frightened and sick.

"Dad?" I said, my stomach clenching.

"Your mother's had to leave with the police," he said. And that's how it all started. How I found out my mother wasn't who I thought she was. How I found out she was someone else. Someone who'd disappeared a long time ago.

Someone who was wanted for murder.